The Monster Within
Dorian P. Belasko

Raven Feathered Books—Madison, WI
ISBN: 979-8-2183510-2-1
Library of Congress Control Number: 2024900472
Title: *The Monster Within*
Author: Dorian P. Belasko
Digital distribution | 2024
Paperback | 2024

This is a work of fiction. The characters, names, incidents, places, and dialogue are products of the author's imagination, and are not to be construed as real.

Published in the United States by New Book Authors Publishing

Dedication

To every boy and girl who has grown up fearing the complexity of their ever-changing mind; through self-love and an empathetic approach, you will find your way.

Table of Contents

Prologue
Birthright

*H*e was a squalling child, even at his birth. His voice rose higher and higher still, looking for affection that he did not deserve. He was a promise, a promise of an Empire soon to be had, and Grace would ensure this child was reflected as such. She stood from where he lay thrashing about and readjusting her dress stepped back to where her row of midwives stood to wait.

"Care for him as you would if I was not present. To not coddle him into weakness," she said, looking to the oldest of the women; gray-haired and lined with age. "I need him powerful."

She left the room to descend the hallway, passing her guard as she did so, turning her head up in disgust at those lowly foot soldiers who had been tasked to safeguard her whilst she was in her home, far from her work. But as she entered the meeting room she somewhat relaxed in comfort, nodding in authority to the advisors that stood around a massive oak table, darkened in age and shining to perfection.

"Acu's current motives it seems is to legitimize the Church in Rome, furthering the rift between the Orthodox and otherwise. But we know this will take him and his family time, already having dispatched some of our own to Constantinople. The only thing I would be more worried about is if the whisperings of the Book of Ages being there. If so, and if found by his members, we would suffer at the hands of his calamities for the foreseeable future. What do you wish to do Queen?"

Grace looked to the man who spoke, furrowing her brow as she listened, slightly snarling her lip at the mention of her long-time foe, Tiraul Acu. But he was the master tactician she had grown to know, so she knew that he himself would never show himself on the field of battle. She looked down to the table, where the small rivets and etchings showed the known world, miniature statuettes of where she had men and women stationed in the world to fight this foe, this creator of all her ill will.

"Send our Hunters to Constantinople, if he has a garrison of men there, you will find them and proceed to slaughter all remaining ties. I want them quashed beneath ferocious attack, Sir. I don't want them closer to the Book of Ages at any time than we are, are there any whisperings of where it could be instead?" Her voice was strong, and her hatred and aggressive tactics were known, *insomuch as to be met by resounding faces of obedience.*

The man shook his head and stepped back, looking to his companions of lore and war as if to ask for their help, instead of being the primary attention of the Queen herself, nervously adjusting the brooch that clasped the cloak around his shoulders.

"No, my Queen," a woman said, setting her helm on the tabletop before leaning forward to inspect the world, gauntleted hands tightening on the edge. She met Grace's brown eyes with yellowish eyes, the scar running across her face always making Grace chuckle inwardly. "However, we are aware of the longstanding garrisons in the city of Roma and more in the country to the east, far beyond our own in Asia. I would ask that I go to those far east countries with my own men and put rumors to rest, and steel to infidels. We must rid this cancer of fear of the Acu's and replace it with that of an unknown entity. The world is starting to separate more than it ever has, and what we do for the next hundred years will dictate how large of a portion we rule."

Grace smiled, nodding agreeingly to the other woman, biting her cheek as she inspected the table some more, unbeknownst to her that she was knotting her fingers together, trying to piece together her decision. Her voice was absolute as she met the woman's gaze once more, a wry chuckle escaping her lips as she snapped back into reality. "I agree, Susan will take her garrison to the east," Grace smiled then turned from the woman, looking to some of the other men who had yet to speak. "You both will accompany Lady Rosa on her travels to the east, ensuring that any and all of your adversaries fall to any sword or hell that you so choose."

As the squalling of her son rose higher in pitch and reverberated down the halls and into this room of war heroes and assassins, they all looked to Grace expectantly, knowing her not as the mother she was. Grace sighed softly, feeling herself biting her tongue and clenching her hands into fists as anger seeped into her face, making her jaw clench.

"Susan, after your victories in the east, you will return and by then, if you are with child, she will join the prince in the cleansing of the world as a Hunter." She looked around to the other men, the heat of anger still biting her tongue. "Too long we have sat and been fought in vain against Acu and his family, for they far exceed our own while we sit and plot in the shadows. We are a dying breed gentleman, and I would no rather, see our numbers dwindle than to die from lack of spreading our seed. We must work on recruitment after the finalization of the Catholics is complete, for soon, when the parting of the world is complete, we will need the bodies to once and for all remove Acu and his breed of Immortals from this world."

She was met with agreeing voices and gazes, and slowly the men started to pound the table with gauntleted hands, Susan Rosa smiling, walking around the table to bend her knee, kissing the Queen's hand in affection.

"Your wish is ours to uphold your Majesty."

They slowly left the room until only the Queen remained; left pondering her next move, staring dreamily at the map, littered pieces of red surrounded everywhere by the pieces of black; Acu's pieces. In one ear she could hear the crying of her son, as well as the cooing of the midwives. Yet in the other, she could hear her blood pound ferociously against her the inside of her head as her anger rose and rose.

This boy was to be the Prince of the Santiago's, Lord of Wolves, and the King to be feared throughout the worlds both known and unknown in replacement of Tiraul Acu. However, she had no patience for the weakness of the child, even in infancy. She knew that he had a long way to go before she would recognize him as her own, for fear of being seen with this failure of a boy if the odds were not in her favor.

She felt a gauntleted hand lay onto her shoulder and turned to see Susan staring at *her knowingly, eyes soft, offsetting the vicious scar that contorted her features, making her more feared than most of Grace's other advisors. She spoke softly to the Queen, but not with affection, but with resolution to the problems she knew Grace was facing.*

"I will solve your problems in the east my Queen, you need not worry on that front. I will return with child, one that will put me to shame even in my splendor so as ensure we might retire from our activities in the field."

Grace sighed in denial as her friend said this, knowing that this fight was her existence. For her, there would be no rest, and until this son of hers rose to meet the mantle of his inheritance, she would never be fully willing to rest from anything, else she would see her world crumble into failure. She looked at Susan, her voice crackling with desperation as she bored holes into the other woman.

"We have been fighting for a long time Rosa, longer still as the family has dwindled in the last few hundred years. The advisors spoke in venom behind my back to the people, forcing my hand to have a child to keep claim on my throne. Yet, what if this child fails to be the willed hand of destruction, I need him to be? We all will be crushed in finality, and all will be for naught."

Susan readjusted the hand-and-half

sword that lay at her side, stepping away to leave the room, turning back once more to look at Grace. She saw the Queen staring at her knowingly, wishing each other luck on their journeys, and fierceness on whatever field of battle they met their enemies on.

"My Queen," she said, smiling softly. A whisper of a voice filled the room. "We have been at this for more than two thousand years, always the literal hand and sword of your family. I have no reason to doubt that this son of yours will be the terror you wish him to be. But you must grow unattached as the simple moments of happiness strike you. For I better than anyone know the pain of losing children you grow to love more so than that of killing."

She left Grace to stare at an empty doorway, her hair starting to slip from the bun it laid in. As the Queen sighed, she slowly started back towards the room the prince had now gone quiet in, ensuring that his care was provided to make him strong, but not overdone to make him weak.

He was the promise to end the war.

Chapter I
William

1070 Anno Domini

He bared his teeth, white and glowing as his face set into a scowl, chest barren as he entered the hall. '*They are all of them, beneath me,*' he thought, looking around to the smaller men and women, their faces meek and lowly even in their older age. '*Cowards, weaklings, peasants, all unfit to be. They must accept me.*' For since the beginning of life, he had been bred for this singular moment and knew that whatever lay beyond the ultimatum of this decision, his life was forfeit of all passions and selfishness.

He was bred to be a King.

As he strode deeper in the chamber, people recoiled slightly in their chairs, and he knew that he frightened them with his appearance. Even at eighteen, William stood heads above the men and women situated in that dark and gloomy cavern, and his rich brown skin with almost black eyes frightened those who had issues discerning him from the shadowy hellscape they resided in. William chuckled in amusement as he came to the center of the circular hall, coming to stand before the Queen Mother, his mother.

His mother: cold and hard as the mountain tops, steadfast and as unconquerable as the sea, her face powered by malice and pain. He dropped to his knees in respect, his head bent to stare at the wet stone below him, waiting for her motion to stand. As it came with a whimsical wave, the room noticeably relaxed, as to assume that he would not still slay them all as easily as he could breathe.

They were the Queen Mothers most trusted advisors and soldiers, longstanding in their positions of power that encompassed all of the known worlds, forever locked in the war of feuding families over artifacts of time and control. These were the men and women who he would one day lead, and one day oversee their usefulness until he decided it had long been spent on their failures. Yet he was her son, and he knew that certain privileges came with his name that made others quake in fear as the stories told. For nobody in this room, save the Queen Mother, was above him, no meek and lowly Lords scared him. He was the prince, and he was everything.

"Break him."

It took a moment for the world to resume

movement in William's mind, for surely, he had just slipped into a daydream. But as he stared at the Queen Mother, he had seen her mouth move, her voice flat as the emotion failed to conjure up, even for her son. Instead, she stared at him in indifference and what he translated as disgust. Her eyes betrayed not even the slightest flicker of care as the confusion riddled his mind, seeping into his bones like the hands now gripping his body. Still, his mind cloudily caught up to the physical plane as he felt the grips and weight of other men and woman grab ahold of him.

This was not what was supposed to happen.

The clothes were torn from him and in a rage he lashed out, clipping a man on the chin as he came back to, surely not going down to whatever betrayal had been laid for him. Yet only more hands grabbed him, binding his wrists in chains, pulling him to the floor on his knees, eyes glaring like the abyss into the stone chair upon which his mother sat, despair and frustration littering his vision.

A man stepped in front of William, drawing his sword across his chest and the boy screamed, choking off the scent of blood, fire boiling like a raging tempest across his skin. His eyes flew open, pain and suffering escaping his face, showing this man before him the weakness of

William. The man smiled, his voice quietly echoing around the chamber making it seem as if he came in confidence as a friend.

"William, this is pain; your punishment for being weak. For showing the world your weakness, and the naivety of life. This pain is here for you to learn. To control yourself, your mind and all those around you. In this pain, you become greater than who you are now."

Another man stepped forward, dragging the blade of his spear slowly, it seemed, across Williams back, throwing the young man forward while spit flew from his mouth as his eyes scrunched tight and recoiled from the hot breath he felt in his ear.

"I am fear, here you will be forced to realize the horrors of the world. In pain, you can be as strong as the fear of all man. Learn this pain, abide by this fear." Before stepping away the man drew his spear rapidly across Williams back, black spots starting to blotch out his vision as he bore his gaze through the Queen Mother, who sat without a flicker of remorse.

Woman and man stepped, one after another, one by one, opening pathways across his body, destroying his mind piece by piece, shattering him from who he had thought he was. The pain realigned him but created something that would never have come to pass and shouldn't. Amidst the torture, voices, and cutting, a soft chime of serenity entered his mind as a voice, a soothingly deep voice that seemed to wrap his thoughts and wanderings in warmth.

They are all weak and lowly, all of them below you. They are rats, shitting in the dark unaware of the prince in their presence. You are a strong boy, now fight!

And then the voice and warmth vanished like a mirage and William focused his gaze on the nearest of his torturers, his bellowing laugh bursting forth, much to the amazement of his teachers and Queen Mother. His eyes scrunched with delight as renewed spirit and endurance entered his soul, if even just pretending.

"More! I am the prince! The Scarred Elder William Santiago!"

In the dark and cold of that chamber, a voice had come to him, saving the fragmentation of his mind from being lost forever, and like the promise of Lucifer, William took from this voice the gift he offered: solitude from the world shattering around him.

Time had lost its sense of meaning as the lessons went on, yet the Queen Mother gave him no respite save water as blood trickled from his mouth, voice raw and ripped from the screaming. Eventually, he gave away the notion that the voice had been a Saviour, instead of knowing it as a hallucination of what was happening, and as such William lost more and more into the pit of despair and desperation.

If only he could free himself from these chains, he would slaughter everything and everyone before finally succumbing to the wounds inflicted on him. Or perhaps if offered a chance to beg for mercy, he would convince someone to help him. Something, anything could be used to piece his reality from this horrendous nightmare.

Was it a nightmare? He couldn't remember that morning at all, and if he watched carefully, it looked as if the Queen Mother wasn't moving in any regard; perhaps this was the effects of a poison or drug from the East, so someone could find the secrets of his family and lineage.

However eventually, while William was distracted in staying conscious, his black locks of hair covered in sweat and blood plastered on his face and neck, a voice stood out amongst the rest.

"Stand him up," the Queen Mother ordered, proceeding to rise from her chair for the first time that night, slowly descending the steps of the well-worn stone to meander to where this pathetic display of flesh lay on the floor.

However, as she walked closer, a slow fire started to build in his chest, growing to a hot horrendous flame, and just as his chains were pulled tight on either side of him, running through stone columns to drag him to his feet, the voice came back.

"Death is too sweet my sweet boy, patience, patience. Wait until you are free, rest and breathe. You must listen for the opening; you must wait for the chance to take your throne. You are a King, so become the King; we are strong. Yes, strong. Pain is easily controlled, let me show you."

She stood before him, face to face, as William couldn't fully support himself, and his black eyes pierced into the brown ones of his mother. She smiled slightly, slowly letting it disappear as if it had been imagined, and slowly seeming to take note, strode around him, studying the various works of her subjects and advisors, nodding approvingly.

Her voice was sickeningly soft, yet not in a nurturing way. She spoke as if she was promising a scolded child the promise of a respite, yet only after they offered her a contract of slavery. She forced him to speak in answering, reciting the answers to questions she already knew. William could see that she wanted him to know she was above him, and that he was nothing to her as he had thought. He was a tool to be used and trained until, Hell granting, the world swallowed her whole.

"William this is the first day of forever. Until you master this all, or until your scars are so labyrinthine that you cannot decipher start to finish, this will be your entire existence. Do you still wish to be a part of this?"

As she reached the end of her question, pausing long enough to let him answer, he could slightly tell another shift in the men and women behind him, as they readied themselves for the negative answer if that is what he provided. William swallowed, looking off to where the Queen Mother stood regal, watching his every move with a hawk's precision, and then slowly nodded to her.

"Good," she said, looking around to her advisors before clapping her hands and turning on her feet to climb back up the steps that led to her high throne. "William, we have tenets here that if broken will cause repercussions worse than death. All orders given are followed, and in time perhaps you can give those orders. But firstly, know that you belong to the Elder now, body, mind and soul. Never betray me, never grow an attachment, and never leave the Elder. Can you follow these things asked of you?"

William forced himself to nod, his legs trembling with fatigue as he tried to remain upright, the cold of the hall seeping into his wounds and causing him to start shaking feverishly, abundantly aware that his life was forfeit.

"Then welcome. Now get some sleep before your training begins," the Queen

Mother said, smiling mischievously as she signaled to someone behind her son and as William strained to look, he saw a woman walking towards him with an iron poker, searing crimson and he turned to look towards the Queen Mother, head shaking as his voice refused to leave his throat.

Finally, as the woman almost reached him, a pleading scream echoed weakly in the chamber as he begged her to beget this vile action on one who had revered her. "Grace!" William screamed as he felt the hot pinch, but quickly black spots became black envelopment as he felt his mind race out of time and space, and he fell into unconsciousness.

However, in the recess of his mind, even when peaceful sleep should have started, William was aware of the soft fear as phantasms of all sorts entered his mind and betrayed him of rest. Instead, he spent the time running and slaying the demons in his mind, knowing he needed to wake up, but fearing the waking world as much as the mirrored visitations in slumber. However once more the voice came, and in his mind, this voice had a figure: a dark and towering behemoth of a man, even larger than William, and where eyes or features should have been only crimson and blue hued flame; his demon.

Chapter II
The Elder

1072 Anno Domini

William twirled the spear through his large hands, bringing it to rest over his forearm as the point positioned itself towards the sparring master who stood with his hands clasped behind his back, inspecting his form.

"Turn your hips, William, move the shaft to the crook of your elbow," he paused to readjust William's arm, having to lift his own arms above his head as he stood much shorter than the younger man.

William watched him out of the corner of his eye, keeping pace with the form and execution, ensuring he hadn't slipped while his sparring master was away. Today was his day of reckoning, after two years of training in all the aspects he needed to work in the field, today was the test of his retainer.

"Good, now push, push, push, cinch, turn and reverse. Well done, now again!"

William turned, listening absentmindedly to the instruction, instead concentrating on the men and women who were entering the stands to watch him. The Elder, more so the Advisors and field commanders than spectators to the event, but he could also see the Queen Mother present, walking slowly next to a woman he had never met before, brown hair wrapped tightly in a braid down the side of her head, hands tight around a sword.

"My Prince!" William turned to where he had forgotten his teacher was standing, scolding William quietly like a boy for going stationery, especially in front of all those he was meant to impress.

"Who's that?" William said, nodding to the war-worn woman still following Grace to her chair, turning her head in William's direction so he could see the grotesque scar running down her face, much like those across his body and he flinched slightly.

"That is Lady Rosa, the Queens most dedicated commander, she has only just returned from the Far East in time to watch the event, my Prince. She is here to see if anyone can impress her enough to work under her command. Now go, freshen up with water before your fellow initiates arrive."

William partly bowed out of respect, repositioning his spear so his hand lay halfway up the shaft, walking to the edge of the pit that had cauldrons of water waiting for those who trained, glacier water that ran down into the tunnels above them, being caught from the walls it would drip from, and William always gagged slightly tasting the sulfur that mixed in with it upon its travels, shaking his head in disgust before emptying the half-empty remains over his head, soaking his chest and shoulders.

A sudden shudder ran up his spine, making him grasp the cauldron with both hands in pain, rolling his shoulders, shaking his head ferociously as he felt the voice starting to pound in his ears.

Turn, look, your prey is entering now. We must pounce on them the moment we are free to do so, no weaknesses. Look at them, so feeble, it is sickening. Kill them now, before they kill you when you are bathing. You will fail if you look away, let me in, let me do this.

William shook his head, fingers tapping his temple as he screwed his eyes shut tight, reaching out to support himself against the wall in front of him, waiting for it all to pass; he simply had to breathe and pay no heed to it. It would pass, it would have to pass, he needed to concentrate.

"Are you alright?" The voice belonged to a woman, who spoke soft as if to ensure only the prince heard her words, and he opened his eyes in confusion, looking down to the woman stood off to his side, offering his spear back to him, having picked it off the ground.

William didn't answer, instead being wary of this new visitor in the pits, immediately looking up to gauge the faces of the Queen Mother and the Advisors, surely this woman was a trap to lower his guard before the event. He grabbed the staff from the woman, keeping his eyes wandering as he started to pace the outside of the pit, walking past small congregations of other initiates, who gave him brash faces with snarled lips, whispering to their comrades as William strode past them, larger than most, both in height and width.

You will crush them, slay them without pause and without mercy. These are weak men and women who are standing in the way of your birthright. Look at them, look at their skin, it hasn't been marred to perfection, they are not royalty William, they are nothings in your way.

William caught himself stealing a glance of where the woman had first approached him, but she had left, and when William quizzically looked around, he found her in the seats above the pit, in front of the Lady Rosa who sat on his Queen Mothers side and he could see the striking resemblance between the two, surely, she must have been her daughter. Her chestnut skin was very obscure in these parts, only a few were seen by William in these halls, yet her hair was black unlike who he assumed as her mother, and shorter, perhaps a foot and a half shorter than he was, thin and small like a doll.

She caught his gaze, catching him staring and after a small moment gave an almost imagined smile to where he stood before shifting her gaze once more across those who were down in the pits with him and William scowled, knowing it had been a trap.

You must not fail; you have come too far. Trails have assailed you within and without, forever testing patience and our fortitude. For that reason, first and foremost, truly you must press forward. If you wish to be the King than act like it, these peasants and traps surround you, always ready to betray you to those who wish your death. Never fall for these traps my Prince, you are made in pain and so only in pain can you be accepted. All else is folly. Bear this woman no mind, she has been sent to poison you from your inheritance.

The master of the pit stood in the center, signaling to the initiates as a hush ran through the hall like a breeze, making everything eerily still as the old man spoke with authority. His voice was cutting as he caught the gazes of all his students surrounding him, absent of affection for those he was charged with training for today.

"Only three will survive the pits today, and for those three, greatness in the Elder awaits you. However, only those immune to the trait of mercy will survive. All bars and regulations binding you to withhold your aggression and skill have been lifted, and in this rite of initiation, you are to kill your opponents or therefore be killed. You will begin when the third gong chimes, and only until you are ceased will you discontinue this artful dance of elimination."

The man ended his words while look straight at William, taking a moment pause as his echoed words died from the pit, nodding respectively before walking through a door on the edge, leaving his students to have a few moments to look amongst each other, knowing that they all were going to become as cruel as they could be.

The first gong rang out and William shrugged off his tunic, revealing the scars covering his body, noticing some of the other men grow cautious and nervously repositioning their stances in his direction.

Those are the weak, leave them for the crows.

Then the second gong cleared the pit as William started to shiver from the tingling in his spine, the voice rising in volume as he tried to calm his breathing, grinding the butt of his spear into the stone. He caught himself looking up to where the young woman sat, void of expression as he stared right at her where she stood with her head cocked sideways, a quizzical look on her face as if able to hear what was running through the prince's head.

The third gong rang out and William spun his body to the left, striking out with his spear to where the slower boy stood closest, driving the head of his weapon through the boy's neck, quickly retracting as the spray of blood issued from his neck before dropping lifeless to the floor. William didn't hesitate before moving onto the next, a woman who was locked in a fencing match with another man towering over her, and walking behind her, picked her up by the neck, snapping it ferociously before throwing her like a ragdoll into her prior opponent sending him crashing to the floor, sword clanging besides him mere inches away from his hand.

William pounced on him with the vigor of a beast, clubbing him maddeningly with his hands before smashing his head against the stone floor, feeling the hot blood of the opponent on his face as anger coiled in his body, adrenaline coursing through his veins as he looked up feverishly, scanning the pit for these next offerings.

Bodies littered the floor, six by the look of it, and while William locked gazes with a boy from earlier, he watched as the boy spun the shaft of a battle axe in his hand, making sure to keep some distance from the prince as he slowly rose to his feet, breathing deeply as he bent to retrieve his spear from the ground, a grimace on his face.

An icy feeling barreled across Williams back as he heard the grunt of another person bringing their sword resoundingly across his back, gouging him open and William fell to his knee in a moment of shock, feeling pain like he hadn't expected to find in any of these adversaries.

STAND BOY, lest you be bested by those beneath you, turn and slay this nonbeliever! Pain is the domain, and we are the master, now spread true terror across these younglings, stand!

William turned manically, lunging to pounce the man, tearing into his neck with his teeth, holding the hand of this opponent with ease, slamming him into the wall where he tore again and again into his neck, spitting chunks of flesh out before letting the body drop lifeless to the floor and turned, his mouth and neck covered in blood, dripping onto his chest as the axed man stood watching, still careful in his pose.

William sized him up as he once more reached for his spear, adoring the pose the sparring master had made him practice daily. He turned his stance, letting the spear shaft rest in the crook of his elbow, ready to go forward into the suspecting opponents' neck or chest, William cared not. The man smiled at William, nodding in a warrior's respect as William snarled, hatred seeping out of his bones.

Before they took another step towards each other, however, another gong sounded, and the Queen Mother stood, raising her hand to those in the pit, smiling brightly at the spectacle they all were allowed to watch, an obvious purveyor of this malic cruelty on one another.

"We have our last three competitors, well done indeed initiates!" She gave an air of fake affection before she strode down the few steps to gaze wondrously at the best warriors of the pit.

William looked around, past the man with the ax to see only a single other; a woman with two short daggers, watching the Queen Mother warily, her hair tousled wildly around her face, still crouching over her last kill, the throat of another woman slashed open, throat partially torn out. William stepped away from the man, circulating the pit, keeping his eyes locked on the Queen Mother as if another trick awaited those she praised.

"Emily," she said, nodding to the knife wielder, the smile disappearing. "You will work with the Elder here, being sure that our abode is kept safe from traitors within and without." She shifted her gaze to the man, then slowly raising her hand to her left where one of her advisors stood at her command. "You will work in the field, we have many wars to win, and a good soldier is a wanted need of the Elder."

As the man bowed before walking away, the Queen Mother caught William's eye, her face now blank as she paused for a moment, scanning him up and down, eyes bright with what he could not place. The moments seem to go on forever until finally the woman behind her stood and walking forward to her side looked down with her scarred face, throwing a rag into the pit beside him, obviously impressed as the smile lighted the room.

"You will be with me Prince, I will caste you to be a Hunter; a member of my battalion that will go to whatever ends of the world we are needed, to sow fear and turn the world to ash if need be. Grab your spear for we leave tonight on your first incursion."

She turned and walked off. The younger woman who had approached William earlier standing swiftly, following behind her, quickly glanced at William; sorrow in her eyes as she regarded him. William watched her leave, memorizing her features and wondering why she had bowed her head in what seemed like prayer.

"Welcome to your task within the Elder, William." Grace regarded him with now cold eyes, studying his shifting movements and gazed attention before he looked away, stepping off to the doorway that would lead to the upper halls, surely to be met with Lady Rosa and her daughter.

The sparring master awaited him, holding poultice and cloth to bind the wound on his back, offering words of praise to the prince, yet William wasn't listening as he sat on the stone bench. The anger had left him, and in its place was emptiness. The voice was silent in his head, and all he could hear was a slight buzzing in his ears as flashes of what he had just done replayed in his head, and he didn't feel like a prince, but like the Headsman who slaughtered all those who could do nothing to deny fate its kill.

"Hello William," a voice spoke from the shadows, and as he looked up, he saw the young woman step forward almost cautiously before offering her hand to William in expectation. "My name is Saige Rosa; I look forward to having you work with us."

The sparring master coughed gently before securing his bindings and taking his leave, bowing to William before exiting the hall quickly, a wry smile on his face as he passed the two in the dark passageway.

William disregarded the offered hand in utter confusion as he sat bare-chested before her, still covered in the blood of the men and women he had just slaughtered as a spectacle for all to watch around him.

"You would do best to be gone from my presence woman, I am not a person you wish to make friends with. I am only here to kill and strike fear in all the Queen Mother bids me to, I cannot be distracted or trapped into your obvious schemes!" William roared, standing to his full height, his brows furrowing in showcased anger, body tightening as he showed his white teeth in the gloom of the dark.

Saige hadn't moved back or shown any expression except that of indifference to the temper that had, to her, sprung out of nowhere. Instead, she simply seemed to study his face, watching his eyes as the silence between them continued, making William seem to wither away in shame of his actions. Slowly she stepped forward, regarding William as she walked to his side, slowly placing her hands on his bandage, asking silently if she might fix it. William said nothing but did not raise an objection, watching her warily as she put her head to the task, readjusting the cloth and tightening the bindings, her brow furrowed in slight concentration.

Who was this woman, unafraid and soft? She did not flinch at his appearance, nor quake at his words. She smiled, and inside him something stirred, confusing him, urging him to run from her, hide or kill. This witch before him quieted and ceased the voices and emptiness that had started since the pit, if only for a moment before seeding doubt and fear inside his head causing panic.

She regarded him softly before stepping back to smile at her handy work. She quite simply spoke, looking at William as if he was a boy that needed a gentle prod into changing behavior. But unlike the malice he was accustomed to, her eyes betrayed nothing but kindness.

"I expect, while alone with you throughout our time together, to have you show the real you. The one you show nobody else." With a small curtsy, she turned on her heels and walked unceremoniously back into the dark of the passageway, leaving William in utter bewilderment as to what had just happened.

This is another trap, my Prince. She is waiting to trick you into a mischievous end, you mustn't trust her. We are one, and what we are, are killers of a carnal nature, she will make you weak and, in that weakness, you will be left empty and open to attack. Scourge her from memory, she will not break the King!

William softly agreed to the voice, knowing that over the years the voice had proven time and time again to be correct, often time seeding out those set to waylay him off his course of birthright, or to try to torture him more and more, to continue the cycle of the Queen Mother. This Saige was not to be trusted, William thought before walking slowly up the chamber, leaving the pit behind him, back aching softly as he rubbed at the blood on his body.

But her smile stained the forefront of his mind, and he couldn't shake it.

Chapter III
Prince & Pauper

1073 Anno Domini

A stooped man stepped out of the doorway that led to the birthing room, his kind and wrinkled hands opening to his sides, smiling to where William turned to face him, moving from the banister he was stationed at, looking down to the courtyard below.

"It is a little Prince," the man started, looking around to where a few others stood around them. The Rosa's, mother and daughter alike, smiling brightly as they started to walk forward towards the door before the man finished speaking.

William, however, did not move. His hand clutching the banister, keeping him secure in place as he looked away, noticing the servants and soldiers alike buzzing like bees down below, going about their tasks as if nothing was amiss.

The next prince was born, and William felt a surge of greed, lust, and control in his body. This boy would soon become his equal, something that William feverishly opposed. Together they would be forced to showcase and share the mantle of power and fear across the world so that everyone would have nightmares of the Santiago's. However, this was William's namesake, and his alone, for a King doesn't share his Kingdom.

"William," Saige's voice broke him out of his daydream, pulling his gaze from the movement below. Turning, he saw her pause halfway to the door and offered him a stolen glance as she noticed that he hadn't moved like the others surrounding them. "Are you coming?"

William took a moment more to remain silent, trying to catch the evading words as he struggled to be polite in how he answered her. The longer he stayed silent however, Saige gave a small half smile, walking towards him, eyes lighting up in understanding as she took his wrist commandingly.

As he begrudgingly followed her, she whispered to him, quietly offering him guidance in the appearance of the prince in the room of the newborn and the Queen Mother. William sighed, erasing the emotions from his face as he set it in neutrality, listening intently as both Saige and the voice in his head battled against each other to have the greatest impact.

"Be sensitive William, this is to be your sibling, and you know better than anyone that this is not a place that he should walk alone in. You must now try your best to watch out for him and not allow him to be schooled in the same way that you were schooled. Be the end of the demented upbringing the Queen Mother used on you. Teach him how to be a prince by purpose, not by the form of fear."

This boy threatens all you have endured so far in your life my Prince. He now shares your inheritance and the promise to steal the Kingdom from you, even if he goes without the proper schooling of what that entails. He will rob it from you while you sleep, crafting plans of treachery to kill you.

He entered the chamber and instantly locked eyes on the little mound of flesh that lay quietly in the Queen Mother's arms, perfectly silent save for the soft coos that came from its mouth, tiny fists gripping his mother's finger only to release it to swat at the air. William took another step forward, noticing the much lighter tint in the boy's skin, his hair a light brown that was matted in little tuffs.

William understood Grace wasn't one to wed men, his own birth was a prime example of this, for the Queen Mother ruled by matriarchy, refusing to let the donor of a man to rule her or the Kingdom she created. However, William took a moment to realize that this *brother* was not in fact from the same line as him. Instead, another man had been chosen, perhaps for the sculpture or blood that coursed through his body, William didn't know.

The Queen Mother already entices to replace you, my Prince, look there, your downfall in the Kingdom in which you sacrificed your entire soul. You are being begged to become the forgotten idol of a world moving too fast for you to succeed in. This fool in the prince's mantle must truly not survive the night, we must rid ourselves of any competition.

"His name is Thomas," Grace said matter-of-factly, showing Thomas to the rest of the room, eyes resting on every one of the onlookers as they all seemed to marvel at this child for something they prophesized.

"A twin," mumbled William, like a child admitting something he didn't wish to, casting his eyes downwards as he started to slowly backstep, into the shadow of the room as the other advisors and guests filled in the space where he had just once stood.

His body started to hum with energy, his eyebrows furrowing as the familiar tingling started to run up his spine and clenching his fists tight, William turned on his heel, leaving the chamber, the thick wood booming throughout the halls of cracked stone. Making it down the flights of stairs that led to the main hall, William was fuming in anger, grabbing his stashed spear as he pushed past the men blocking his way from the front gates, surprised faces turning back to a fleeing William, too preoccupied to notice the quieter footsteps falling behind him.

He needed to beat something beneath his hands, to feel the crushing and malleable skin and muscle give way to his torrenting hatred and seething murderous rage. He needed to put another in pain so that he himself could gain control of everything: the feelings, the thoughts, voices. He needed to command everything in his body and mind, so he could prepare to conquer all aspects of his life.

You are destined to be alone, forever my Prince. Be prepared for this, and command those around you. Give no heed to the paltry circumstances that try to conjure up the substance, they are nothing. This child is just another obstacle that you will get beyond, focus my Prince, we have much to do together.

William cocked his head to the side, feeling an eerie coolness that sprinkled the edge of his vision, like a miraged realm, a cold sense of understanding bursting through his moment of sanity as he saw his demon watching him. His eyes pierced him, out of the corner of his eye, like a cat; they seemed to follow William in judgment, knowing the fly is nothing to fear. William flinched, as if shocked by giving attention to his physical consciousness, as if he wanted to keep himself secret from anyone who might be watching, as if he didn't enjoy being the one watched, even if it was only William himself.

My dear boy, you knew when you accepted me in, that I would become what you couldn't dare achieve on your own. I promised you reprisal from the bill of darkness, and in turn, I must stay, not in the recess of your mind, but as your equal, always aware of your thoughts, your words, and your actions. I am here to spectate the world through your eyes, and you are here to rule by the actions of my choosing.

The sudden confusion and sea of downtrodden pain were unbearable. William staggered over into a stone column, his spear dropping from his lifeless grip as the world spun around him, mouth open yet unmoving as he begged to breathe.

An outlet for that pain must be had, and only one cure exists for pain and misery unjust in its dealings: revenge; rage, in such a manner where woman flee, children plead, and men create nightmares.

'To be named a Monster,' thought William, shaking away the voice paralyzing him as he tried to stand to his feet. 'Caste as a demon and consulted like the devil. To ensure the Histories remember me, in all of my magnificence until only snow or ash cover the world.'

So enraptured in this world was William,

that he hadn't noticed the footfalls that had stopped echoing behind him or noticed the airy voice calling his name again and again. At the simplest of touches though, he was pulled back, like the snapping of a bird's wing and the world realigned until he realized he was drenched in sweat, on all fours like an animal staring off into the distance.

He felt her hand, gliding from his shoulder up to the nape of his neck, lightly rubbing his scalp through his tangled hair. "Are you alright?"

Three quietly whispered words, and Saige still hadn't moved. And then he noticed that her fingers were making little circles in his hair, mildly relaxing him. Him, the man who hadn't been offered physical touch as a means of kindness until she had come back out of the suddenness. At that moment, in the dark horrifying taste of punishment from his mental captor, William was utterly defeated, however, Saige held such terrifying beauty at that moment that William caught himself breathing in, his lungs thanking him as they expanded, white splotches covering his peripherals.

"Yes, I must not have had enough food to eat today. Care for a bite before we go out again?" William stood, snatching his spear as he stood to his full height, bearing himself to those that were catching his eye, snarling slightly as he continued forward, yet when William didn't hear Saige move with him, he turned in confusion.

She was staring at him, a mixture of somberness and pain crossing her face as she stood still as if she was trying to process something that was in the forefront of her mind. Her voice came out matter-of-factly, straightening her posture as she stared at William dead in the eyes as if facing an oncoming horde of enemies as she made her final stand.

"Stop getting in your head William, I asked you to be honest with me."

William flinched away, confusion crossing his face as he stared at Saige warily, waiting to see if she continued yet when only silence echoed between them, he shook his head without saying anything, as if, if he spoke, the truth of what had transpired would come booming out of his lips, condemning him to the title of insanity.

"I wasn't, I told you, must have fainted from lack of food." He laughed a hollow laugh as he turned, walking away down the steps, hoping to outrun the piercing gaze of Saige before people started to notice what was transpiring.

"I saw your face. You make a face when you're in dark thoughts and try as you might hide it faster than I can realize, I saw it. You lose all the emotion in your eyes."

William stopped dead in his tracks, staring ahead of him where in the distance he tried to pretend to focus on the bustling peasants in the fields, or the home-guard, standing watch from the parapets. How did she see so much?

The one who tries to get between us will suffer the fate of what should have befallen you deep in the cavern had I not saved you. The Hell of old, where fire and brimstone surround you, smog choking your lungs as you feel the presence of a multitude of devils, knowing that you cannot outrun them. She cannot know of us my Prince, play the part of Royalty, no one shall know you.

A whisper fell out of his mouth, eyes cast downwards in defeat as he placed one foot in front of the other, walking away from the specters of his blight as he spoke now to his demon, voicing the fact of what he knew was coming as he felt the tingling run up his spine again, a hot metallic taste springing into his mouth as he clenched his jaw to keep his teeth from jarring.

"Now, run. For the beast returns. I never truly know what he does, or what I am doing." Breaking into a brisk walk, William scurried hurriedly off, leaving his imagination to soar as to what Saige must have thought.

Yet the prince had more pressing matters, he must remain strong and steadfast at the moment. The Queen Mother had sent them on the task of pooling citizens of her Kingdom, for they must be ready for her

next move to ravage the lands of the
Israelites. Of Jerusalem. William smiled.
Ferocity came back to his face as he
imagined the sowing the tare from the
wheat that were his enemies, gripping his
spear more tightly as the knuckles of his
hands paled in comparison to the flush of
the skin in excitement.

Chapter IV
Oath

1200 Anno Domini

William slowly entered the clearing in the wood. The dew of morning running across his doeskin boots as he treaded carefully, letting the moment get noticed in all its glory. He readjusted the pitch-black mantle that lay over his royal purple tunic clasped with a crimson brooch and belt, the finest cloth that he had ever worn, for today was the day most important in his history. He wouldn't let the rags of a pauper ruin his standing in the eyes of those looking to him.

As he stepped forward, his brother Thomas was waiting to meet him, a head shorter as the curls that seemed so soft as a baby now curled down to his shoulders. Squared jaw giving way to a much more thoughtful countenance than William could have expected.

His *brother* was a peaceful soul, one that William was mildly off put by. Everyone referred to Thomas as the diplomat, the negotiator, granting him the title of silver tongued; there was never a seat at a hall empty while he was present. Yet William regarded him as an inferior species, knowing that at the end of the war, there would always be a battle to win, and a fight to have, save you expected defeat on the battlefield.

William was a soldier however, and the chaos, the war, the death, all these things had become the man, and he them. Without them, William was lost, confused and even more tormented than usual. William had thrived on such pain, such a singular purpose, for to kill, to save and to hide everything in-between became his saving grace from inner conflict.

"Are you ready my brother?" Thomas urged him, having noticed the vacant expression crossing the eyes of the elder brother, smiling coyly as he assumed that nervousness had rattled William.

Let man suffer in silence, for the waggling tongue causes strife.

William no longer bowed and bent whilst the voice interjected. A long hundred and thirty odd years had normalized him for the consistent opinion of his phantasm, and agreeing softly, William moved Thomas aside with his arm, disregarding the younger man as a wolf regarded its prey, moving even more to the center of the clearing.

"Be gone," said William, the venom in his

words making Thomas recoil as William walked forward, adjusting the decorative sword that lay on his hip, rub encasements seeming to shine with the morning sun as it filtered through the thickness of the forest.

Time had turned him bitter and sour, like an overaged wine improperly stored. Yet he did not care. Little now influenced him to care; instead, he strode forward, passionately aware that the fire he had had when he was younger had seemed to pass. In its place, knowledge, and apathy for anything not taught as a core value.

Yet the thoughts running amok in his head ceased as he focused on the silhouette in front of him, for there stood the wonderful sight of Saige; beauty encapsulated into form. Even from here, against the cream of her gown, William could see her freckles lining across her face, the grey-green eyes gazing at him with an understanding; a certainty and promise of truth that he had never witnessed anywhere else.

Before William stood an unmatched beauty to anything he had seen in his immortal life, and he knew that smile, that laugh, and her words of comfort would be something that he would endure and always seek after for as long as he lived. She had shown him loyalty and love, casting down his demon and ripping away his walls in every moment of the long years they had come to know each other. For her, he would soon caste the demon out of his head altogether, for too long he had allowed it to remain. For her, and his love of her, he would succeed.

Her hair lay in ringlets, and William sauntered forward, his vision tunneled only on her as if chasing through the gray of a dreamscape, wanting and needing to be sure she was truly there, as the perfection he knew her to be. His heart swelled with each passing step, and the fire in his body was different than normal; for it was stoked in love and admiration to the point where even the voice of his nightmare could do more than idly sulk in the recesses of his mind.

He watched her smile light her face, dimples carving into her skin as he watched her eyes twinkle with understanding as he marched obsessively to her, hands reaching out to reach for her face. But a slight shake of her head reminded him of the ceremony and, arms automatically dropping to his side, William came to an almost crashing halt as he realized he was almost in placement, never noticing the Elder strewn behind him to ensure the ceremony happened in the standards of the Queen Mother.

He flushed a deep red, one that luckily nobody would have seen, save Saige, and slowly continued forward, back straight as his eyebrow raised, nodding to the Master of Ceremony that stood by Saige, his expression blank yet ancient. As he spoke, a cackling whisper broke in vibrato across the opening, and William shuddered, smiling slightly to Saige as he watched her expression, studying how she reacted to him.

"We are gathered this morning to celebrate the joining of these two in matrimonies and to give them our blessing as they gin their new lives, joined in one vision and one purpose."

Silence littered the onlookers, and William had to tear his gaze from Saige as he turned towards the decrepit old man, hands held out, his palms facing up as he looked steadily back into the eyes of a man set for deaths embrace.

"Brother Santiago, do you give your word that you will teach your children to be moral, virtuous and to seek truth?"

William boldly stated that he did, not moving an inch as the ceremony continued, echoing his agreement with each passing oath, the old man inching slightly closer and closer still, making the hair on William's neck partly stand as Saige stood and watched.

"Will you teach your children our ways and continue to guard our secrets?"

The onlookers all spoke in unison, their voices shaking the air around William, "We are nothing if we live without honor.”

“As a man, my word is my honor, and as such, it shall be kept.” William replied, feeling Saige move closer, almost cautiously.

The Master of Ceremonies spoke once more, producing a blackened ironed spike from within his robes, offering it to Saige, his face still blank as she took it, hesitantly looking at William, who nodded, affectionately smiling as he looked back to his palms.

“The world invites deception, punishment awaits the wicked. The heart of man is darkness, yet it is we who must guard the light. Now these secrets shall be passed on through this family. So, let us make it known that two have our blessing and our protection, and through the Wife does she bind the Husband to his word.”

Saige placed both of his hands on top of each other, setting the tip of the spike into the soft flesh of his palm, ensuring it was straight and staring deep into Williams eyes, her eyes slightly watered as she almost recoiled from his gaze.

“As a woman, my allegiance is to the truth, and as a wife, my loyalty is to my husband. Let this action show conviction to the truth, and bonded loyalty to the man.”

William smiled, bringing his forehead down to hers as their noses touched, a soft purr springing from his chest. He could smell the rose oil in her hair and felt her joy and utter happiness through the vibrations in the air around her. William opened his eyes, only briefly, to stare down at the woman who had no inkling of the amount of love he felt for her, yet still gave her entire soul to the one who was meant for her. How he loved her; slowly he kissed her forward, smiling to himself as he felt a tear spring into his eye.

Then with a fluid motion, William could hear the Master of Ceremonies bring down the heavy hammer to the spike that Saige still had unmoving, steadfast against his hands, and with a bright flash of pain, William was brought to his knees, in front of his wife Saige, hands held in the semblance of prayer and contrition, now bounded by pain and blood.

"Through all trials, does my love prevail," William said, smiling up at her as she wept, hands wrapped around his face as she knelt before him, coming down to where he had stooped.

"Through all trials, does my love prevail," she repeated, before leaning in to kiss him, pulling the spike back out of his palms, letting them fall to his sides as she giggled out of joy, kissing him smartly, and passionately across every inch of skin she could see, as the onlookers cheered triumphantly.

But in all those moments, William was

simply in awe.

For before him, was his existence; his perfection, and his wife.

Chapter V
Asher

1500 Anno Domini

William sat back into the pews, on the right side of the Queen Mother as Thomas sat on her left, the Prince and Usurper, thought William as the filtering of voices in the chamber climbed to an annoyed level, making his back rigid as he ground his teeth in frustration. He had always hated these gatherings, when one would join the Elder or rather, seek an audience with those who circled about the hall to garter favor. He preferred the old methods, the methods that he had been shown when he was a small boy; through pain are all things made perfect.

As William settled back and the voices came to a grinding halt, the caverns hall boomingly echoed as they were opened, and walking in, William watched as a pale skinned boy entered, surely fresh born into the world of war, with the eyes of innocence.

The voice of the Queen Mother was direct, void of emotion as it usually was, and for once, William smiled knowing that the boy in front of the hall would cower as the coldness of the tone reached him, aching him to the bones. "Asher Valentine, I presume?" William snickered to himself as the boy looked around, gazing at the faces throughout the hall, eyes settling on everyone beyond William, and the Queen Mother, with a subdued malice in her voice continued forward, past the blatant disregard from the visitor. "I asked you a question youngling; are you, or are you not Asher Valentine?"

His voice was reedy, and William raised his face away, disgruntled as to how disgusted the boy seemed to make him. *He is a pathetic tool standing amongst the Gods*, whispered the voice, and although William wasn't the world's largest fan of the rest of the Elder, he could not help but agree as this specimen seemed to be the bottom of the rung amid those he had come to see as the greatest masters of his time.

"Yes, Milady, I am Asher Valentine, the same who sent you the letter requesting that I could join your group."

A hiss broke across the room and William watched as the boy flinched slightly, and William coughed in his throat, bile rising as he leaned forward towards the Queen Mother. He was rarely one to speak about matters that she could easily have figured out herself, but with someone not deserving of the title that they had all fought hard for,

William felt it was his right. She didn't even turn in his direction, but instead cocked her ear as she continued to gaze forward, his voice too low for their guest to hear.

"This boy is weak, he would never past the old trials, look how he portrays a beaten dog. We mustn't allow him in."

The Queen Mother made a noise of agreement before leaning forward herself as the boy stood up slightly taller, face nervous about the outcome of judgement. "And who, Sir Valentine can you name as family that is already included in our ranks?"

William's face scrunched up as the voice whispered to him, causing him to stand as if shocked with electricity. *A pestilence to the Kingdom, an insect beneath your boot, END HIM.* Instead, Williams' voice boomed across the cavern, the power in his voice shaking with anger and power. "One that is high ranking of course. For if your family is that beneath the lowest of ranks demanding respect, then you would not even presume as to come here."

Williams' eyes flicked as the door to the cavern opened slightly, a hooded figure entering briskly, unaware of the boy in the pits. William watched warily as the newcomer arrived almost silently, the Elder watching without speculation as the man walked silently behind the boy, who was staring blankly at the Queen Mother, almost as if the words in his throat had closed on him. It was at that point in time that William had an idea who was now introducing themselves, and a grimace of hatred spread across his body.

"Benjamen Essence Valentine," the voice said, and William sat back in his seat, annoyed that Valentine had brought his boy before the Elder. He was pale-skinned, and William hated those who were like him. Proud in a weak sort of way; but the Queen Mother favorited Benjamin for his proclivity of killing, and Benjamen continued, purposely, it seemed, to not look in William's direction.

"Sorry I am late Grace. The duty you had me fulfill took a little longer than I had anticipated. I am profusely sorry."

William watched as the Queen Mother nodded towards the one that had come from nowhere but had gained through the ranks seemingly with ease. William growled quietly as he folded his arms across his chest. Here in front of him was a person that had called the Queen Mother by her first name, something that he had never seen done before, except for Sir Valentine himself, and not something that he would expect to see in the time after, or from someone else in his stead.

Benjamen continued, the pride in his voice conjuring up and William scowled, leaning forward. His voice was rich and deep, and even William could not doubt the regality that was behind the voice. "I speak for Asher Valentine in this hall as a reference. I am his father and as I hold the position as one of your closest advisors, I will hold the position of teaching Asher our ways and punish any clumsiness that might occur."

William sat with bated breath. Before him stood a member of the Elder that he personally did not like. Seeming to draw from a memorized script William listened as Benjamen recited what seemed to be a quoted passage, and the furrows of his brows deepened. This boy had a pale face and speaking for him was another that William did not like. The Queen Mother was not particularly fond of those that spoke greatly of their position, but this was news that William already knew. He smiled as he watched this pale boy snicker in continuation. He thought that he was above all that William held dear, but how wrong he was.

Next, the Queen Mother spoke, the coldness in her voice was apparent.

"No, Benjamen. I will not have you teach Asher. I will have William do so, for in our ranks, we will not have biased people. William, do you agree with me with what I ask of you?"

William leaned forward, eyeing the boy in speculation. Oh, how had the times changed so much, that now before him, he was asked to be tasked teaching a beaten pup on how to be the nightmares that kept mankind awake at night? He internally growled, knowing full well that all he wanted to do was to kill the boy in front of him, but he would showcase the raw power needed privately, as to not be banished from his future Kingdom. *Hunt him until he succumbs to the pressure of the world he is entering, let me show him what being a Hunter really is. Release me.*

William leaned forward, covering his face to conceal his scowl and took a moment more to answer, as he tried to see what this young man could hopefully turn out to be. "I do your Grace," smiling internally as he saw Benjamen scowl on the play of words. "Your wish is my command, as it always is. I will teach the youngling."

William saw Benjamen and the entire encirclement of listeners relax, some even breathing out audible sighs of relief. He smiled once more, for now this boy knew what true power was starting to look like, and the fear of who William was, was surely running amok in the boy's mind. Finally, the room was silent once more and William leaned forward precariously. Next was the new test of who could join, the power, and the talents. The reason this boy who stood thinner than a bamboo shoot, could still hold the various skills that it seemed more and more to dominate and filter into the world.

The Queen Mother spoke, if she was hinting or cautious, it was well hid, for while everyone else stood at attention, and even William prepared to pounce, she remained as barren of emotion or interest as her voice came questioningly. "One more thing then. Is there something else you can do, something that would put you at an advantage when fighting others of our kind, or even your kind for that matter?"

A shiver ran up William's spine as the anger and hatred spiraled out of nowhere, causing his mouth to salivate, fingers dragging into the stone arm rests of his chambers chair. With a twitch of the lip, William watched as the boy said nothing, looking down and closing his eyes, and his vision tunneled on the boy. He felt like he was being watched, and the voice venomously seemed to watch, like a cat in the corner.

He sees us, he can see our mind, kill him! He goes to be a puppet master to play the game of chess. He can see us!

William scowling, slowly starting to stand as he watched the boy raise his hand for a moment, hearing the Queen Mother shift for a moment before they both opened their eyes, and the boys voice echoed across the room for the first time, in confidence and splendor.

"Yes Milady, I do."

Grace stood, waiting for Thomas to follow suit as she smiled for the first time, making William glower even more, before ushering them down from the pulpit to meet the boy face to face. Her voice seemed happy, and for the first time, William could not detect any falseness in her joy. "I welcome you to the Elder, Asher Valentine, and I place you as one of our Wise Guides. Will you fulfil the duties of that position, until death takes you, and abiding by all our customs?"

William watched the boy nod, and William shrugged off his tunic, his scars shining in the dark chamber, the low light seeming to illuminate them, and he saw Asher glance over as he was walking up, sizing up the prince, noticeably gulping away his fear. As he stopped a few feet from the boy, he spoke, knowing that he had his undivided attention. He spoke low, voice gnarled and gritty as he watched Asher follow the scars from his chest to his neck and face, then back down, seeming transfixed and petrified.

"Take a good look son, your kind and your people are easy to kill, and my body is the roadmap to how."

He smiled, baring his white teeth as he watched the boy in front of him turn a slight shade of red, seeming to square his shoulders as if anger was directing his actions. But, as the boy seemed to take a step forward, and as William smiled joyously in his head, the voice excited to kill this insect, he felt a hand on him.

"My name is Saige Santiago; I am William's wife."

William relaxed, letting her speak on his behalf, knowing that she was everything, he was not. As she introduced herself, his mind drifted as he watched the reaction of Asher looking up at his wife, and then, as they appeared, Emily Damus and Lucian.

The other pit survivor had only gotten fiercer and more direct as she spent more time in the Elder, and William always enjoyed having her present, for when she was present, he felt as if he was not the only monster in the room. The old initiates were always those he felt shared a bond with him. Others, like his wife, or Asher were usually accepted by birthright.

He watched silently as Asher had people introduce themselves, noting the occasional phenomenon, such as causing Lucian, someone he despised as much as Benjamin, to go red and fluster himself about, smiling to himself. As the two made ultimatums, William cackled, watching as Saige gave him a sideways glance, before William took the boy by the arm, much firmer than what was needed.

"Asher has no part in the Elder if he cannot kill, so work must be done." William started walking the boy through a door, smiling at himself as he knew that he would break him.

Chapter VI
Santiago

1509 Anno Domini

William sat in the corner of the room, the dim light of candles dancing across the stone floor and walls, lighting his skin as he wished to hide even further in the shadows. On the bed, Saige was strewn before him, a countenance to be sure, but a countenance distracted. He watched her smile, eyes lighting up in unparalleled joy, her voice bursting out in childish laughter as the baby next to her continued playing with her fingers, babbling nonsense in an all too quiet room. As he continued to watch her interaction with their newborn son, she caught him staring, and William stared back at her, no emotion lighting his face until finally she gave a sad soft smile and continued once more with their son.

"I am trying you know," William said finally, voice soft as he bore holes into the wall in front of him, refusing to meet Saige's eyes now as he spoke, feeling uneasy.

"I know William, it just hurts sometimes."

He could feel her eyes on him, and then complete silence enveloped the room, leaving nothing but the voice to watch him, off in the distant recesses of his mind.

William looked down, unable to find purchase with any singular thought, instead having a tumultuous wave come crashing through him, as he wrestled with the voice in an endless array of violence and splendor.

Now you are bound. The glory of an immaculate death will evade such a Prince as yourself.

William closed his eyes, turning his head to the left, recoiling slightly. Before him was this little handful of flesh that would soon be his replacement in the world, yet William felt no love for it, no passion, and no loyalty. Only disgust and anger. Wasn't that how he was taught? That through pain, only perfection came forth; and this boy was a showcase of how he had not completed his training.

He feared for this child's existence, but not for the world, or from sickness and disease. William feared for him because he was unsure of just how far this voice controlled his actions and mind, and at the end of the night, William was a killer, without reason.

You shall have power and dominion over all things my Prince.

The voice conjured in his head again as

William watched the child start to fuss and squirm beneath Saige's loving touch, her gentle and soothing voice cooing him as she picked him up, resting the baby on her chest as she gazed deeply down at him, William forgotten in the corner.

He wasn't meant to be a Father. He was raised to be the Scarred Elder, the nightmare that kept men awake at night; a monster to shadow the world. Yet before him was something that pulled his mind even from Saige, and for the first time in his life, William felt a wave of fear of failure pass through him. However, a coiling of anger and passion rolled up William's spine, throwing him forward for a brief moment as the vibrations rocked into his jaw, opening his eyes in frenzied delight.

You're a survivor. Many came before you for the purpose of ensuring that you succeeded. Don't take the chance of sacrifice for the allure of willingness. That would be a waste and a shame to fall to the allure of fallacy. This boy is beneath you, and easy prey to the predator. Rise and go see your Kingdom.

William stood from his chair in the corner, and Saige stirred from her accidental slumber, the baby boy asleep on her breast, eyes closed with a peaceful countenance. As Saige fully woke up, clear eyes gazed upon William as he watched their son, and she smiled, reaching out to

William, gesturing him to come closer, a twinkle in her eye.

As William strode over, he sat on the cold stone floor beside the bed, watching Saige and their son as she lovingly laid her small hand on William's cheek. As he closed his eyes, conflict ran through his body once more; on one side lay anger and the voice, and on the other, unease and fear. For, laying before him was a child dependent on him.

"We are keeping him William," Saige said, her voice absolute. "You must promise me that you will not send him away to grow up with an army of midwives. You have to be present as often as you are able."

As he said nothing, she leaned up in the bed somewhat, touching her forehead to his, silent once more as William sat without a word, brow furrowed.

"Your past mustn't hold your future hostage," Saige said, kissing him gently, her voice barely more than a whisper. "Your tormented past is why I know our son will have a wonderful life. You are the final apple to fall sick from the tree, and now that you are healing, so will your son come from a generous tree. Love him like you love me, William."

William nodded, looking down at the boy, running his thumb across the small apple cheek of the baby as he continued to sleep against his mother's chest. William smiled slowly, hidden in the shadows as he once more watched the small pound of flesh make no movement to the affection William was showing.

"What do you think he will become?" William looked back to Saige, a smile flickering across his face as her eyes searched his happily, as she kissed him once more, holding the lock as she seemed to convey her deep love for William.

"If we are lucky, something like a painter, and if not, a bread maker." She giggled as William picked the baby up from her breast, holding him to his own chest, sitting on the bed next to his wife.

He felt a stirring in his chest unlike anything ever before, and he looked sideways to Saige, and in return, she gave him a reassuring nod and smile, rubbing his back slowly as William continued to gaze at this little ball of life, still unsure of how it came from him.

"His name is Christian," Saige said, pushing the boy's hair out of his face, which was black like Williams.

"Christian Santiago." William sighed heavily, noticing the voice in the back of his head pinching his thoughts in a vice-like grip, but William only brought the boy closer to his chest, noticing a protective feeling coming over him.

For all that he was, and all that he was going to be, one thing was for certain. Even if William was due for a hated past and a damned future, his son would be safe and sound, so far out of this hellacious landscape that he would dare to be anything he wanted with such a passion and freedom that he would never know the nightmare he was meant to live in.

Chapter VII
Queen Mother

1650 Anno Domini

"I heard they offered us her body as a means to secure peace. They said that they didn't know who she was, or else they would have never set upon her with the ferocity they did." Thomas spoke, looking down at the Queen Mother, seeming to be saddened as he gazed at her beyond her black veil.

The chamber around them, however, was almost empty, and William didn't say a word. He looked down at this woman who seemed too impervious for death, that now as she lay in deaths embrace, seemed a simple joke played on him. This torturess and master tactician lay here just bones and pounds of flesh, unable to will the world to her ways.

"They knew who she was," William said, his voice dead flat as he looked away from the Queen Mother, instead walking past where his younger brother stood over her. "The reason she is dead is because they knew who she was. Do not be so naïve to assume they wouldn't strike in war Thomas."

William walked passed where Saige and her mother Susan stood a few feet away, garbed in black, eyes watching him as he stopped and stared at the onlooking Advisors of the Queen Mother, fully aware that the Elder now fell to one of the two Santiago brothers, and absentmindedly, William turned partially to face Thomas, who in turn, was still watching the Queen Mothers' body, downcast in despair.

"The Queen Mother is dead," William's voice reverberated throughout the chamber, he squared his shoulders resoundingly, a light buzzing filling his mind as he looked to men and women scattered about. He could feel Thomas turn to face him, quizzically unsure of what William was doing.

"Tiraul Acu has brought this century long feud to a resounding finish," the chamber was silent.

William watched as the Advisor stared at him, and in the back, huddled in the dark, was his old teacher. The man who had prepared William for the Pits, and by extension, war, and the Elder was so haggard and frail now, but William could see a spark in his eye. With a quick smile and nod, the old man stood, seeming to want to get a better view of William.

"Now we will go to war again, but this time, you will follow me and whatever paths

I bring us to. This I swear to you, that the death of the Queen Mother will not go meekly by. She gave us all task and purpose, and today, that purpose is renewed; we will hunt down every rumor, every shred of the Book of Ages, and in that process, we will slaughter and erase any and all memory of those who stand in the way of our exaltation. We will come from the shadows now, to show our enemies why they should have never forced us into the light."

William was met with silence, save the few who pounded hands onto the wood pews they stood up from, only for a moment, to nod encouragingly to the prince. However, it was short-lived.

Thomas stepped forward, almost touching William's elbow, but deciding against it, addressed the chamber, William behind the younger Santiago. As always, his voice rang out, catching the attention of everyone in the room, diplomatic as ever.

"The Elder as always is burdened by grief at the loss of life, and even now, when our Matriarch lays before us, we already speak of war without end, a suffering blight in the histories of empires. Grace was a wonderful leader, a Queen of us all, through and through. However," he paused, glancing back at William, a somber expression on his face. "To break custom for revenge of any sort is exactly what we must not do. We have customs to take this to a vote from all the Advisors and the Santiago's of who is to run the Elder now that the Queen Mother has passed. So, go, break bread and share wine, and as always, we will continue to do what we do best, which is ensure the safety and peace of our families and our friends. The future of the Elder must be bright, so bright it will be!"

The chamber erupted in voracious pounding as men stood and rose their voices for Thomas, who in turn smiled, stepped down to walk amongst them, back to William as he walked to the door leading out of the chamber. Only a couple stood behind as Thomas and the others left, and William didn't show any emotion as he saw his teacher in the back, along with Susan, Saige and Emily walk to the front of the room, standing before William; the four horsemen of the apocalypse.

Susan spoke first, stepping forward to the prince, dropping to a knee, the scar on her face knotting in her old age. "I swear my fealty to you, such as it is Prince. When the Queen Mother saw an enemy, she sent my Hunters to eradicate all traces, as you very well know. Let me follow through on my tasks for you and rid those who would seek for the elder of the Santiago's left in the world. I will bring great victories as I have always done for Grace."

William smiled, helping her to her feet as

he laid a heavy hand on her shoulder, nodding as his voice came out low and menacingly, looking at those in the room.

"All things uttered in this room stay in this room. The time for all our lives to be wasted has come to an end," pausing, he glanced at Emily and his old teacher. "While we are away, I need people here who will ferret out stinking ranks until my Kingdom is free of spies and traitors. Whether by plotting, treachery or murder, this Empire will not fall into the weak hands of one who would see us flitter away to the unknown parts of history."

You are the King now boy, slaughter those of your people who would stand in your way. You must slaughter your brother, kill him while he sleeps, and gouge the eyes out of these ill-bereft advisors, they do not wish for you to take your throne. You must take your birthright by force!

William agreed, listening absentmindedly to the four in front of him discussing plans in hushed whispers as the prince started to stride towards the door of the chamber, softly running his thumb down Saige's cheek as he passed her.

William asked the voice for power, to ensure that everything was taken care of in the coming weeks, months and years, for he knew not where the blades would come from to stab the prince in the back and end his reign before it all started.

Trust nobody. Everyone who knows you is afraid of what you will take from them, so they are all ready to betray you the moment you turn away, you must end them. Start with that pale skin, Lucian, we must drive him off. Let me take the reins my Prince, just like that.

William felt someone grab his arm, and pulling William from his head, he spun, grabbing the assailant by their throat, lifting them high in the air like a child held a doll, eyes looking unseeingly into the face of his old teacher who gasped for air, frail fingers trying to pry William's off his throat, feet kicking weakly in the air.

"William!" Saige screamed, starting to run from the front of the chamber, but it was too late.

Just like that my Prince, rest while I weave my web of power for you in the Kingdom.

William watched through what seemed like a gray veil as Saige stared at him mortified, a lifeless body at his feet, neck snapped, and eyes puffed out as they stared into the wall to his left. However, William didn't speak as this dream like landscape eluded his ability to come back from.

He smiled, or rather, his voice smiled.

He saw the pain, true pain on her face, and even then, the light didn't flicker. *This is power my Prince, true power. Do you see now, how you cannot feel the remorse, or the weakness of death anymore? Truly you are a monster to monsters, a truly scarred and magnificent viSaige of carnage. You have allowed me safe passage and now, the monster has been let out, at last.*

"Now," said William out loud, staring blankly at Saige. "Run, for the beast returns, and I know not what he does."

Saige reached out and grabbed William's face, pulling roughly as she tried making him stoop. Her voice was deadly quiet, barely more than a whisper, but her eyes glinted in anger and love at the same time, teeth bared white.

"Are you the manifestation of the voice?" Saige's eyes bored into his, cupping Williams ears as he smiled.

"I am a King, and it is by death that any man, woman or child meets their night when they lay hands on the King," the voice said, William watching the reel of his life like one out of his body, making his mind shiver with a frenzy.

"Your name is William Santiago, and I am your wife. Man and wife, love and love, through all time and some after that. You are not a King but a man, wounded and hurt who needs to focus."

William jerked back, a snarl coming to his lips as he pushed Saige's hands away from him, watching her face flicker in fear as she took half a step back, hands slightly raising as if to fend off the behemoth of the man that stood before her, twisted and dark in his coldness and anger.

"If I am not a King, then you are no Queen, and just so, insects are being crushed beneath my feet. Leave my sight!" The voice roared, baring teeth before turning on his heels, grabbing the chamber doors and flinging them open with an anger that reverberated through the wood and stone of the building itself, jarring his teeth. He was the monster within.

The sun smacked him in the face, and grimacing, he looked around to where groups of spectators adorned in their black garment of sorrow stood or sat, watching William Santiago, the Scarred Elder, walk amongst them after the death of the Queen Mother.

As one man approached him, wearing a disgustingly false expression of affection on his face, the voice snarled once more in William's tongue, grabbing the man by his face, fingers gouging into his eyes as he turned and hurled the man at the column of stone behind him, spitting on the ground before looking to the horrified people before him.

The voice recited, conjuring up a memory William had forgotten long ago, bile rising to the front of his throat. The voice boomed across the courtyard, transfixing everyone who was looking at the prince. "I am fear, here you will be forced to realize the horrors of the world. In pain, you can be as strong as the fear of all man. Learn this pain, abide by this fear."

"What are you doing?" Thought William, voicing conservations to his demon. The voice chuckled however, pressing on, manically feverish of tearing apart every soul not loyal to him.

Chapter VIII
Inheritance

1653 Anno Domini

Once more William stood in the pit, almost six hundred years after the first time he had been initiated into the Elder as a boy, and even now, William could feel the age-old blood and sweat upon the dark rock surrounding him. The simple lights that cast a damned hue over this deep and dark place made his eyes droop with exhaustion; as the years went on, William's rage, and the voice's presence sapped his strength from his bones.

Thomas stood ten feet to his right, chin up as he stared up into the stands, hands uniformed behind his back as he unwavering stood resolute, not even giving show to Williams' presence. The King smiled before he too looked up to where all the remaining advisors of the Elder stood in blackened clothes and armor as they took turns walking up to the bronze cauldron on the top of the wall that separated them from the depths of the pits where the brothers stood.

Every so often an advisor or field commander would give an accidental look towards William or Thomas, before hurriedly looking away and moving on, hood hiding their faces in what could have been guilt or shame. William saw his wife take her turn to the cauldron, pausing to look down at the two brothers, eyes flat as she seemed to regard them both as nothing more than bickering children.

Long ago had Saige given up on quieting the voice that seemed to take over for the King at times, for when the beast came out, always came the nightmares for all who stood in the path of wanton destruction. William cared at moments, and he felt his heart pang, however it was often short-lived before the beast came prowling back to the front of his mind, ready to once more takeover to ensure the protection of his host was continued.

I told you, did I not? In time, the truth of loyalties is always showcased. Now you can see that the only person who has your interest most at heart is me, my King. I came to usher you from pain and woe, and over the years, that bond has only been strengthened. You see me as the demon that you are stuck with, but we both know that you love the feeling of power, above all else, you are a Machiavellian King.

William rolled back his Shoulders, feeling the humming of power start to rise, and he grit his teeth, grinding his feet into the floor, locking eyes to where his son Christian took his turn at the cauldron, making a quick vote before turning away, and William smiled as others got out of the way of his son.

Finally, when all the votes had seemed to be place, Susan once more stepped before the onslaught of decrepit old men and the younger generations who were ready to take their place after the earth turned them into dust. Unsheathing her sword, he hurled it into the pit, where it landed between the two men with a clang, skittering to a halt, and the room was silent as they waited.

Susan spoke out, her voice booming down into the pits as she regarded the brothers, gauntleted hands resting on the stone as she seemed to regard them with an air of confidence.

"The person who picks up that sword claims the right of the throne, to be a King of the Elder. However," she paused, looking at William and Thomas, one than another, watching them. "Should you pick up the sword meant for a King, only to have the Elder not cast the majority votes for you, then you must be forthwith banished from the Kingdom, along with all those who voted for you. Decide the price you pay for royalty."

William turned to face Thomas, and the shorter of the two brothers smiled, moving a strand of his curly hair out from his face. He took no step for the sword that lay between them, but instead kept his eyes locked with Williams, trying to read his thoughts it would seem, as William watched his brothers' eyes dart around his face, brows furrowing in concentration.

He knows that his time has failed my King. He knows he is lost, look now, see how his fear is catching his body in a fright. Pick up the sword and gut the worm who would wriggle at the feet of one such as yourself.

William smiled to Thomas, not saying a word as he strode forward, grabbed the sword by the handle and reached out, pointing the tip mere inches away from his brother's chest, where Thomas looked down, then back to his brother, a deep sadness coming out from his eyes as he gave a half smile, cocking his head up to where Susan stood watching, nodding slowly for her to continue with the votes.

"The votes are from thirty of those that you have trained with, studied with, fought with and depended on for advice, wisdom and insight. Now, they will dictate which of you is King. William, since you have picked up the sword, if you are the victor with the votes, your brother Thomas, and all those who vote for him will be cast away. Do you accept this responsibility?"

Susan's voice was gruff, but William nodded, feeling his grip tighten around the sword as the voice whispered in his mind, begging to be released, to caste the votes himself by killing all those who knew were against the King from when he was much younger. He begged to be let out and wreak havoc in this world of dwindling men.

The brothers watched as Susan filtered through the coins that had been deposited, separating them on the left or right side of the cauldron, as nobody spoke around them, and William kept the sword pointed at his brother, just in case he was wrong.

We will not go so easily into outcast my King; we are the very embodiment of the Elder. We will kill them all, down to the very last person who will stand in our way of absolute power.

Christian and Saige shuffled to the front of the group of hooded figures, taking place on Susan's right hand side, looking down at their Patriarch, who watched them, giving a wink as he watched one side piled higher than the other, and William felt a burning in his bosom of triumphant success. He was the King, now, plainly before all that had ever come to know him. Now he had gained everything he ever wanted.

"William is triumphant, hail to our new King!"

Thomas fell to his knee, head bowed to William in a gesture of respect, as the hooded figures drew their swords, all save Susan, as they lowered them towards

William, who in turn raised the one he held to them, spinning from left to right to match each of their gazes before laying it before his feet, smiling broadly.

His breath deepened as he gestured for Thomas to stand, turning to address the cavern of onlookers, his voice thick with emotion as he realized the mantle, he now wore in front of them. King, William, the Scarred Elder, stood before them and now he was set on the path of greatness.

"Who voted for Thomas," William said, voice loud and ominous.

We will kill them now; banishment is too good for them.

Susan looked somberly down at William as she listed off three names.

"Lucian, Emily Damus," Susan paused, for the first time looking hesitant, and fearful. William watched Saige walk up to her mother reassuringly, laying a small hand on top of her shoulder before looking kindly down at the coin she held in her hand, and she froze in horror.

Even from this distance, William could make out the movements of her lips as she voiced the name without sound, turning almost maddeningly slowly towards her son who was staring down at his father, eyes blank as his jaw was clenched, hand laid on the pommel.

"Christian Santiago," Susan seemed to sputter past disbelief as the advisors around her gasped, starting to whisper to themselves, and Thomas stood next to the King, once again regaining his regality in diplomacy.

He betrayed you. The Pauper betrayed the King, and in doing so, took his very own prince from him. Let me out.

William closed his eyes, dropping to his knees as he covered his ears, bile coming to his throat as pain seeped into his bones and tremors started up his back, making him spasm quickly, catching himself on the stone as his face contorted into a painful nightmare as he stood up, turning towards his brother, a snarl on his face as he bared his teeth, lip trembling in hatred.

"Wait, no William!" Thomas managed to get out before William took his brother by his throat, walking him into the wall of the pit, lifting him high above his head as the voice took over, venom and hatred wracking his body as he trembled and shook in the sight of Thomas, heavy breathing coming from his nose as he looked up in disgust, grip tightening.

"You are everything beneath me," said the voice, watching as Thomas fluttered against the Kings behemoth strength. "In betraying the King of his son, you shall be hunted and slaughtered; your days haunted by the thought of me finding you in the dark places of the world. Now, begone!"

Thomas tried escaping the grip of William

and the voice, but was instead dropped to the ground like a lifeless doll, and William turned, staring up at his only son, snarling in disbelief, the distance between them seeming to stretch as everyone around Christian parted like the sea, giving no hinderance to his father glowering up at him.

"I, King of the Elder, banish all those responsible, and forthwith deny them privileges or access to the Elder, under further penalty of death."

William watched as Lucian gave one last look down on him, a wry smile on his face as he parted, Emily following Lucian without a backward glance, a pang in William's heart to see another pit survivor leaving him. Finally, Christian seemed to slow his exit, glancing once more at his father before leaving for his banishment, holding onto his mother's hand for one last time, giving a somber look as he too exited the pit, for the last time, seeing William, the newfound King of the Elder.

Saige looked down at William, and the voice stared back at her, untrusting of her countenance as he strode to the beginning of the steps that led to the advisors who now stood ready to follow his every command.

When he reached the top, William looked down to the empty pit to see the scuttle marks of where the elder brother had dragged the younger across the floor and sand, and smiling, looked to the field commander who had served the purpose long before even he was born.

"I want these strays hunted down, they must not share the secrets of our sacred order, and I would trust nobody but you to ensure that this is the case. I will not have my kingdom fall into ruin because of four individuals who might see its end due to jealousy."

He looked past Susan where Saige was watching him, and he smiled lightly, walking past her mother to lay his hands on her cheek, smiling down at her as the voice promised him absolute loyalty from all those who betrayed him.

Chapter IX
Cuba

1653 Anno Domini

William stood on the forefront of the ship, the sea's air pushing his long hair from his face as he shut his eyes to the breeze that swept past him, cooling him off. The men on deck gave him no heed as they kept the ship on course, sailing towards the island mass in the distance, and William internally stomached disgust as he saw the sandy shores and deep rich trees of Cuba. He has never enjoyed the heat, or the humidity.

As William turned, Asher caught his eye, saying nothing as he continued sharpening his knife on the stairs that led to the main deck, his hair all around his face.

"How do you want to do this my King," Asher said, venom pooling out of his mouth as he spoke to William.

William said nothing at first, looking back to the island once more, pondering their next move. It was here that the trail of the Book of Ages had led them, and so with noble rights, William was the one to secure it. Leaving his kingdom in the care of the Queen in his stead, William pulled with him his hunters, along with Asher and Susan, the latter of which stood by the Helmswoman.

Your new Prince seems eager to please you, my King. See how fear has brought forth your replacement son, in lieu of your traitorous firstborn. You have all that you have asked for, and now, the greatest history is about to come at the closing of your fist. Oh, a glorious day for the King of the Elder.

William smiled, walking past Asher, gesturing for him to rise as he started towards Susan, who looked down from the helm, nodding as William made eye contact with her as the trio made their way to the captain's quarter, leaving their hunters to continue their mindless task of getting them to their destination.

They gathered around his desk, all three falling into overstuffed chairs as William regarded each coolly, fully aware that these were the best the Elder had in their ranks, and that today would be a swift victory. As he watched Asher regarding the King out of the corner of his eye, Susan too watched William, the corner of her mouth pulling up into a grin as she kept the silence, waiting for the youngest of the three to give up in annoyance.

"So, what is the plan tonight, Sire?"

Susan chuckled as William leaned forward in his chair, smiling back at her as Asher broke the silence, confusion crossing his face as the two battled veterans broke out in a silent joke amongst themselves. Susan spoke first, giving them all a brief overlay of the rumors she had heard that had initially caught the attention of the Elder, to ensure they were all on the same page.

"Our agents have tracked the Book of Ages to this island for us, and its guardian. It is surrounded by humans and one changer who has been with it for years supposedly. The humans guarding it call themselves Dragons, who," Susan paused, looking at Asher expectantly. "You might remember crossing paths with over a hundred years or so in Istanbul to dispose Suleiman the Magnificent." to which Asher nodded, staring at the desktop.

William chimed in, picking up the compass in front of him, tossing it between his hands as he kicked his feet up on the desk. "There are also the usual kingdoms on the island, so we should have an easy time to come in and leave, we just have to be quick, and not stay longer than a night if needed. We don't have time for getting into the drama over the lives of these humans, so we will beach, and conquer to divide. Susan, give us the details of our prey."

Susan straightened up, collecting the

figurines on the desk laying on the map of their destination, starting to scatter them across the island, organized in their placements. Without missing a beat, she started reciting, drawing the two men's attention to the various pieces as she spoke.

"Here is the encampment of the humans who have made a home here on the island. They don't know about the book, but they do guard the stray Changer who protects the book. My agent tells me she overheard him speaking about immortality, and his friend's ability to share it with a lover he has taken; and even mentioned Asher himself."

Asher sat up quizzically, looking at the aging woman, asking without words who mentioned the pale skinned hunter by name. Susan looked unperturbed as she continued, looking at Asher, then to William, seeking his advice. "A changer such as us William, who guards a book, yet is a Stray? Who has friends who can change someone immortal, but speaks ill of the Elder? This man must come from Tiraul family, and we cannot let them have that book."

William gazed at Asher from the shadows, expectantly as Asher smiled devilishly, nodding to the King before Susan continued, watching the two men's silent interaction.

"My agent has her men on the shores, but

this is where the dice begin to lose their certainty. These humans calling themselves Dragons breed a great sense of loyalty, if they weren't our enemies, I honestly would consider them as applicants for our human guards, but alas," she broke off, staring at the pieces lost in thought before shaking her head and continuing.

"The men on the shore are a mixture of those she knows answer to her, but they at the same time don't fully know that she works for the Elder, specifically me, instead of the human *King* back on their home island of Port Royale. So, we need to ensure her safety if she becomes a target. In doing so, we can have the book come to us, along with the ring that coincides with it."

William stood, laying his hands on the corner of the desk, examining the table of pieces with a scrutiny and treacherous foreboding. He said nothing as his jaw knotted, brows fusing together as he seemed hard in deliberation.

"What is the agents name, how will we know it is her?" William asked, grabbing a wooden pawn from the table, not even glancing up to Susan.

"Samantha," Susan said quickly. "Small woman with blonde hair, has a dragon tattoo wound up her neck."

William nodding slowly. "Asher will go for the Changer; you will kill the animal and rob him of this book. I don't care about this agent Lady Rosa, I care about the secrecy of our kingdom, and our efforts to rule the world. With that being said, this little bird of yours is not to make it off the island, regardless of what she does or doesn't bring us." William paused, straining his back as he moved his finger across the beaches on the southern part of the island. "This is where you will beach with Asher, to depose the Dragons and the Changer alike to grab the book." Moving to a beachfront a few inches away, he continued, voice low. "This is where the hunters and I will beach. We will push forward to the camp to come on them unawares while we secure the key."

Will you allow me to come out to play my King, let me grab your destiny for you. Let me bear it on a tray of skulls and gold as your divine right to rule. Let me out to feed off the blood of all your enemies, known and unknown.

William flinched, pushing the voice from his mind.

"Asher, you are not to leave the Changers side until he is dead, even if that takes fifty years. Follow him, follow his lover, and erase all men from his family. That is the task you are forthwith tasked with until the end is nigh. Do you take this task from your King for the kingdom you are a part of?"

William looked up to see Asher staring at William, a mixture of disgust and jealousy on his face. Asher nodded finally, standing to go prepare his gear for his extended travel, leaving the quarters to the two older, Elder members, each regarding each other in both respect and cautiousness. Susan was the first to speak, standing from her chair, looking up, albeit barely, to the King, eyes flickering across his face.

"You share your mother's ferocious mind, my King. She would have been proud to see all that you have become."

William curled his lip at the mention of the Queen Mother, and he saw Susan frown quickly.

"The Queen Mother was many things, Lady Rosa. However, she was nothing like me." William regarding Susan coldly, his anger starting to rise as she refused to back down.

"Nonetheless, many in the Elder are fearful of you my King, you must not let that fear die. Even from my daughter," Susan paused, reaching over to grab William's hand affectionately, and for some odd reason, William didn't recoil.

"You and she were promised to each other long ago, and the fact you two grew into love means the world to a mother. However, you were tasked to rule a Kingdom for the rest of time, should the late Queen have moved on from this plane; not to cater to every whim. You were the first and only hunter to be trained as you were. We created the monster to kill the monsters, and none shall bear your liking again. You must do justice by the existence you threw away, even if that means throwing away my Saige for her protection."

The voice reared in William's mind, greed and jealousy stabbing into him as William took a step back from Susan's hand. *We made you what you are my King, not these old women. They ruined the art they were trying to create, and we came and patched you up, made you into what you see before your very eyes: the Prince, the Lord, the King and the Monster. All bow to you because we will it so, and that is all. Don't listen to these lies.*

William disregarded Susan's speech, staring into her eyes as he didn't blink. "When we reach the island, I want all those you deem guilty of treason to fall to your sword, can you do that for me Commander?" Susan smiled, bowing, turning to go, yet the King continued. "This is a port, for the trading of human lives if I recall correctly. When I leave with the ring or book, you will stay behind and start training or weeding out human tributes for the Elder. Should the time ever come where I want a disposable army in these evolving times, I will call upon you, my most loyal Commander, to send me an army to be in awe of. Dismissed."

Susan turned on her feet, after bowing once more to the King, exiting the quarters quietly, leaving William alone and in silence, save the rocking of waves and men above him. He sat down back into the chair, rolling pieces around between his fingers as he let his imagination loose on the coming hours and days that lay ahead of him and his subjects. He had forty hunters with him, but only one other changer, and then a pale skin. But his hunters were the disposers of kingdoms; war and famine awaited wherever they went, and they never failed the King, nor Lady Rosa when she preceded his rise to the throne.

If they have many men on the island, we should intermingle with our hunters. Send some of the most loyal and undistinguishable to the island tonight, under the cover of darkness to steal their uniforms. Mimic the tradecraft of Susan with her agents, lay traps for all those who try to outwit you, my King.

William agreed with the voice, eyes still glazed over with the far-off daydreams of chaos and violence. He caught himself thinking of his son Christian in his exile, and that of his wife, alone in the deep caverns of the Elder, probably cursing the King for the machinations of a madman.

We are not mad my King, we are powerful; you are powerful. More powerful than Asher with his violence, or Thomas with his words. We are more powerful than Susan and her spies and Emily with her treasonous ways.

You will be the King of everything you wish to see laid before your eyes, bent and submissive to the Master. Let me out and make it so.

A knock issued from his door, and William came to, commanding the guest to enter, not moving from the shadows of his chair as Asher reentered the room, a pack slung over his shoulders.

"I am ready to go at your leave. Is there anything else you would ask of me? Or am I simply to track the changer here, grab the book, and destroy all the men from the family he interacts with?"

William smiled, opening a drawer to the desk, pulling out a red leather-bound book, rubbing it, lost in yet another memory. He walked up to Asher, handing him the book, and taking it, Asher flipped through it, giving William a quizzical look as he laid bare its empty pages.

William laughed, laying his hand on the younger man's shoulder. "In your adventures, this book will maintain a record of all you come across, all your prey. When a hunter goes deep into the lair of the enemy, he must be sure to keep his allegiances straight, and his violent side out to play. Do not be mistaken, you are a dhampir; a half breed of a pale skin, and as such, your tasking you are undergoing is no meager task. You will be set upon on all sides, both from Tiraul and his family, and the strays exiled from the Elder, and you will be so deep into the hunt, that you will not receive any help from the Elder. From this moment on, you are alone in the world of monsters, so notate all that you deem precious and keep your mind."

William gave a final smile, an honest one, as he ushered Asher to leave, watching him close the door behind him quietly, standing still in the dark quarters as the voice waited, slowly advancing on the King, as if to usher him back with honeyed words.

"I know, I know," William said mockingly. "Let me out."

Chapter X
The Ring

1653 Anno Domini

"**A**re your men in position?" William stood by Susan in the dark, the creaking of the ship loud as the moon shone off the water, the island shrouded in a thin layer of fog, seeming to tendril across the waters, threatening to climb up their ship in some sort of witchcraft.

He could hear her readjusting her sword at her hip, her armor clinking; metal aged from before even this generation were but thoughts in the minds of their many. Yet still, Lady Rosa always wore her armor, like a history to the testament of loyalty to the kingdom. Her voice was but a whisper in the wind, Commander and King, alone upon the decks as they watched the landscape of their hunting ground.

"Yes, my King, we sent them to their points hours ago, by the morning, they will be integrated in the soldiers who answer to the Dragons. Your victory will be swift and absolute. Will you go ashore alone, or do you require the advanced guard?"

William said nothing, scanning the horizon silently as he readjusted his own sword; the sword of the King from the Elder, albeit unpreferred to his own spear, William had to carry it now. The breeze hit his chest, and he breathed in deeply, the ocean seeming to yawn as the ship creaked, lapping against the water.

Looking up at the moon, William's mind wandered slightly, wondering if his Queen was outside looking at the same moon currently, the distance between them further than it had been for over a hundred years, and a soft pang made his heart ache as he finally looked to Lady Rosa, shaking his head, hand on the hilt of the kingsword as he paced alongside the edge of the ship, hearing the men slowly clinking in the dinghies down below him, hushed whispers hauntingly echo up to him.

The commander spoke from behind William, and without turning, William stopped in his movements.

"I expect this will be the last time we see each other then my King," the older woman paused, but still William didn't respond or move as he waited for her hesitance to pass. "When you go back to the Elder, will you pass my love off to my Queen? She will not understand to what lengths one must go to abide by duty and loyalty. She has a kinder heart for that, one that I fear might break if she doesn't get closure with my leaving."

William spun; his brows creased as he regarded the Commander awkwardly. Was that normal? To carry warm lies as wishes to those who wouldn't be able to comprehend the truth behind the words. Surely, even one as such as his wife would rather the truth, beyond her own feelings? However, all the King did was nod, closing his eyes softly in understanding before he caught a flicker of a smile before the night shadowed her face as she set her helm upon her head, bowing to the King.

"Thy will be done." The Commander turned on her heels, swinging herself onto the ladder that led to the boats that would ferry her, and later, him, to the shore.

William watched as the men accompanying Lady Rosa quietly transversed the water towards the shore, one by one disappearing into the mist, the noise of oars mute as they seemed to ghost themselves off into the unknowns of time. When the last boat finally escaped his view, William sighed heavily, leaning over the side of the ship, looking down into the dark water, transfixed by its hidden depths. Now here was the mystery one would never solve, the King thought as his eyes watched the furling and curling of the water, climbing and dancing around itself in a hidden language.

"We are ready for you Sire," came a voice

off besides him, and William turned to see one of his Hunters gesturing down below where his own boat and men were being prepared to be sent off. When the King didn't answer, the man continued, clasping his hands behind him as he looked down in servitude. "The helmswoman is prepared to leave upon your return, we are all ready to act on your word."

They think you are slow; look how they dote as if on a sick horse. Show them the Monster.

William said nothing, nodding instead to the man as he walked over and started the climb down to the boat below him, looking back up where his servant was following him, finally feeling his boots touch solid wood once more, lowering himself to the front of the boat and standing up to look at the shore. He could hear as more men settled into positions, making way for the larger man quietly as they pushed off, slowly starting towards the shore.

"It will be some time before we reach our rendezvous spot Sire, are you sure you wouldn't be more comfortable sitting while the journey continues?"

William turned to see a younger boy looking back at the King, sheepishly going red and William said nothing, looking back towards the island, rigid and absolute as the other boats around them started keeping pace, and William could feel his nerves start to itch as a rolling power coiled up his spine, saliva pooling into his mouth.

Something didn't feel right, but William couldn't place it, trying to shake it from his thoughts as the hours drug by, the boats winding around the curves of the island, the sun rising slowly. As it started to steady out however, William still hadn't gotten rid of the ominous feeling that seemed to dominate his mind, and his heart started to beat faster than normal as he caught himself scanning the tree lines and shores in front of him as they continued on.

You need your release my young King, if you do not let me out, you might feel my effects. Let me out and let me calm all your worries, for we are strong, and no King should be worried about the finale of their heritage. Today, the Scarred Elder shows the world just who we are.

William shook his head visibly, telling the voice off. He clenched his jaw as his hands tightened around the sword at his side, yet his hands were sweaty, and William looked down alarmed and quizzical, opening and closing his hands as he gazed down to see the beads of sweat conjuring on his palms.

"What is this," thought the King as the voice seemed more urgent in his desires, the boats docking into the sand, Williams Hunters jumping out to prepare themselves on the shore, William still on the boat. This was a feeling William had never experienced

before in his immortal life, and his stomach knotted as he growled, jumping into the shallow water, closing his eyes as he showed his face to the sun, breathing in deeply as he tried controlling his body.

You must not be weak.

William jerked his eyes open in surprise, anger rising to the forefront of his mind as he heard the voice seemingly over his shoulder. William was the King, the victor of the pits, the Scarred Elder and one of the most nightmarish visitations that this world had ever come to bear witness. Who was another to state that he could even be weak?

You are no King in the eyes of those that will see you act as a boy, watch as you learn what you are truly capable of.

The clanging of steel brought William back to, and he looked up, seeing blood misting the air as it seemed to hang above his men in a cloud, their voices crying out as something beyond the Kings view was crushing into him. Smiling, William started the slow walk forward, drawing a vial from his coat as he drew his sword. Pulling the stopper out with his teeth, he slowly started coating the kingsword with the clear liquid, careful not to let himself touch the poison that was usually reserved for torturing prisoners of war.

OUT!

The voice roared and William crumbled to

his knee, dropping the vial into the sand as he was forced to catch himself. Slowly he stood, grimacing as his nose crinkled in disgust, telling the voice once more to be gone as he readied himself for combat. The voice seemed to hesitate and prowl around the corners of his mind, like a large cat waiting to pounce on an exposed weakness.

As William broke through the forefront of his men, he stared at a man facing away from him, drenched in sweat and blood as bodies littered the sands around him, a giant broadsword at his side, arms hung limply in fatigue it would seem like. The man seemed uncaring about the tip of the sword in the ground. William watched as this man turned to face him, eyes deep with wisdom even from this distance.

William had to admit, he was quite the specimen, standing just as tall as the King, another behemoth of the man, but still young and small, and so outmatched. However, William regarded him now as a foe, slowly letting his eyes fall to the sand, smiling softly as he felt the power humming up his back. This must had been one of the dragons that the Commander had spoken about before, and how right she was, for before the King, lay a human that he would have crafted into death itself.

Let us play.

Looking up, William released the broach that clasped the dark cloak around his shoulders, letting it fall into the sand. He watched as the young boy before his scoured the Kings body, watching in confusion as his eyes set on the labyrinth of scars shining in the sun, a sadness seeming to cross his face, before catching William's eye.

Let me out!

The voice tore into William, and as William blinked, the voice took over, rage and hatred rising like a horrendous wave across him, baring its teeth, a monster before the man, jaw clenching. The voice pounced forward, closing the gap between the two men in a single stride, bringing up his sword to battle with the adversary, chuckling maniacally as the younger man only barely managed to bring up his own sword in time, crushed beneath the voices and the Kings forceful strength and passion.

Yes, yes, yes, now this is fun, kill him we shall! Watch and watch some more as we beat beneath us this unworthy foe!

Again, and again the voice laughed and swung the kingsword fiercely, beating and besting their foe step by step and William watched in the gray mist of his mindscape as the opponent was gasping for breath, his eyes flickering not in fear, but in total understanding of what was going to happen.

William roared at the voice, and suddenly

the voice released him, watching him as if the puppet master cut his strings. For surely the King was still in control of the voice, and not the other way around. For he was the monster created while the voice was the monster within.

William turned without a word, walking back to his discarded cloak and broach, and without a word, some of his Hunters stepped around him, throwing it over like a mantle for their Liege. William nodded to the opponent, who stood ten feet away now, gasping for breath, seeming to straighten up with a second wind.

"Who are you?" The man spoke, pacing around, cracking his neck as William watched him switch sword hands.

William nodded off to his Hunters, signaling to make their way to prepare the boats, there was nothing for the King here any longer that his disciples could not get for him, he would wait on the deck of his ship while these young humans were toyed and tortured, the King had no sport in those being so far out of his scope.

When his Hunters started walking past the King, William stepped towards the man, lightly twirling his sword, smiling. "A person, just like you. However, unlike you, I belong to no meager master. I answer to no meager Lord, and none here shall get in my way, for I belong to someone who has the world in her hands."

William saw the flicker of movement, quickly rising to meet his sword, blocking the broadsword that swung from a now revived Dragon as the young man roared, his voice loud and commanding as his face scrunched in concentration. "Then I shall slay you and lay you to rot in the earth!"

William blocked another attack before bringing his foot up, kicking the man hard in the chest, sending him flying back, the man dropping only momentarily to his knees before standing once more, digging his feet into the sand, eyes rolling back in his head as the breath was forced out of his lungs. William strode forward, happy that his prey didn't go down so easily.

"Do you think you can stop me? I belong to a world far beyond your comprehension. I come here for a sole purpose, one that has nothing to do with flesh and blood." A glimmer in the sun caught the Kings attention, and glancing down, he saw an obsidian stone lay on the man's finger, a dragon sketched into it. The key to the Book of Ages was before him, and William gazed at it more intently, a growing sense of lust washing over him.

"Dragons and Numbers mean nothing to us, for they can do nothing to us. We come for artifacts that mean more then you have come to know." William leaped forward, twirling, spinning his sword as he sliced into the unprepared man's chest before standing still, watching the man's reaction curiously.

The poison was a fast action one, and William only had to wait a single moment before the young man looked down, staring quizzically at his chest as the gash started to bubble and froth. William reared back his arm, throwing his sword through the air as it impaled the man with such force that the young man fell to the ground, paralyzed.

The King strode forward, slipping the ring off of his opponent's finger to place it on a chain around his neck, dropping to his knee besides the dying young man, watching his fear-stricken eyes as they watched the King with the realization that he was utterly helpless before such power. William whispered down to him, laying his hand on his shoulder.

"My name is William Santiago, a monster beyond your wildest dreams."

He smiled, turning back towards the ship, feeling the weight of the ring lay against his chest. In the distance, William heard cries of pain and the ringing of steel and the sharp burst of gunfire, and smiling even broader, the King stepped into the boat that awaited him, ready to conquer all the others.

Chapter XI
Thorned Roses

1684 Anno Domini

"You must not let this quest for the book, ruin your life William." Saige's voice was soft, her hand laying weakly in his as she eyed him softly from the bed, beads of sweat dotting her forehead. "You must find who you are, just as you promised long ago in our vows."

Williams knees dug themselves into the stone floor as he stared at her face, trying to memorize every flicker of her soul that ran the length of it, mere inches from where his wife was succumbing to her wounds, dying, where she would leave the King alone in the world.

Without looking up, William tried to speak, his mouth opening and closing but to no avail, the air itself trying to remain in his lungs. Finally, with a nasty sound, a raking gruffness barely whispered throughout the room as he addressed the healers around the two, huddled so close in the throes of death.

"Leave us."

With small shuffles, William and Saige stared without a word at each other as all others left the room, closing the door with a soft clink, and the silence between them was deafening.

"I am a child, Saige." William bowed his head, resting his forehead on the edge of the bed, screwing his eyes shut as pain seemed to ache into his bones. "I am a child, lost in the labyrinth of my mind, with naught but a candle in the enveloping darkness. I cannot escape this prison, more so if you leave me now."

He felt her hand softly on his head, fingers running slowly through his hair, her nails scratching his scalp and he hummed, feeling a momentary ease as his breathing calmed. The two seemed to sit just like that, for hours as William forced himself to relive the memories he had with his wife in their long life, trying to remain steadfast in the despair.

"If there is anyone to find their way out of the maze everyone crafted for you, it would be you alone my dear William. You are the most loyal and fiercest companion I could have ever hoped for; you must remember that only you can be your Saviour. You must promise me."

Why couldn't people see what he was so anguished over? Here, laid in front of them, was a small whimpering, tortured child, with a ripped apart mind and shredded soul. With a beaten heart, he saw this child that his mind had left, and nobody stopped to care. Enveloped in their own worlds of Heaven and Hell that they had no time to save this child from his.

Even now, watch as her promises fall forfeit. Watch how even she, the one who promised to care and watch over, even she is now so prepared to leave you as the twisted and foul creature that you are. With her time falling short, now truly, nobody will bring you back to who was taken into that pit as a young man. Only I can keep him safe, my King.

"William?" Saige spoke again, cooing as she lifted his chin up, telling him to open his eyes and look at her.

William opened his eyes, staring in silence into hers. He could feel his lip start to quiver, and biting his cheek, he shook his head softly, trying to control his emotions, but his wife laid her hand on his cheek, stopping him. A single tear escaped his eyes, and his soul felt like it shattered into a million pieces, a tidal wave of despair seeming to be like a floodgate, washing over him as wracking sobs bent the King with an unparalleled weight.

"My poor William," Saige said, her voice cracking as the man grasped at the wood of the bedframe, fingers ripping into it as he growled, feeling her hands on his shoulder.

You have given her everything, and

confessed the supposed innocence of your soul, yet all you reclaim back is the painful truth that everything I told you is true; you are unwanted and doomed to be alone.

No matter how hard William tried to convey his admiration, feeling that he knew the entirety of the world used him as a messenger for, still it was not enough. He loved her, yet she was now leaving him alone to the world. To her, he was nothing, nor would be anything that she needed in life. He was a discarded tool in whatever machinations that she deemed necessary in her own games.

Yes, my King you must remember, she plays you like a harp. She makes you promise to find what we have hidden, yet is she not now abandoning you? Calling you weak?

The voice cursed, drowning out William's thoughts, cursing and spitting, turning his love into anger and hatred, and William was conflicted. William stood with a sudden movement, towering over the bed as he looked down at his sickly wife, who in turn watched him with concern before realization conjured onto her face.

"William, focus please, come lay with me, tell me your best memories of us." She reached out to him, offering him a hand and smiling feebly.

William hesitantly watched her, feeling unsure as the voice played in his ear, whispering as he gestured to William's wife. Still Saige held her composure, grabbing the Kings hand, squeezing his palm softly twice before running her thumb over his as she watched him above her.

Through pain, are all things made perfect. She has played you King, and now she is about to show you pain.

A shudder seemed to run up Saige's body, and William watched as she momentarily closed her eyes, grimacing as a soft whimper ghosted on her lips, her nails digging into her skin. William growled, sitting on the edge of the bed, using his kerchief to wipe her head.

"You should have never gone outside these walls without me Saige, you should have known that Tiraul and his family would see you as a target. You should have-" However, he was cut short as he watched his wife shake her head, closing her eyes.

"I wanted to go out because I will not be a slave to fear William, you know that is not who I am. That is not who you are either, or who we taught our son Christian to be. It is in my nature to feel the world talk to me through nature, so walk in nature I shall do, whenever I please." Her voice didn't chide him, but her grip in his hand tightened slightly. "Besides, those Assassiyuns met their demise by the hand of my guard, and the man you hate to admire, Benjamin Valentine. Had they not been with me on that outing, I most certainly would have not made it back to you, but only because they were, are we here, talking now."

These beasts use poison, just as you do, to show you how they can get to you. They take from you your distraction, because you allowed yourself to be blinded by something you yourself cannot fully comprehend. You do not know love, yet it is in this folly that you lose the person you deem to care about, to the simplicities of poison. Fool.

The voice swelled inside him, growing larger and larger still, until finally it grasped William, wrestling with him in his mind with such the likes that William had never experienced before. Standing once more, William paced to the window, holding himself upright, placing his hands on the wall on either side of the window. As he tried to breathe, the voice cursed him, throwing him under a shroud of black, as a pain in his head started to erupt, making Williams' neck start to have pins and needles.

A racking, deep-throated clawing sound filled the room, and William spun to see Saige staring at him, one hand reached out to him, the other clutched her chest, eyes lighting up with a glow that the King had never seen before. He watched, paralyzed as her eyes focused and unfocused as she seemed unable to take a breath, before finally, with a strangled cry, she called for him, her voice pleading.

"William!"

William bounded, yet not even as his first foot landed, he watched as Saige crumpled, as if all her strings had been cut. Eyes unfocusing off of William, her outstretched arm collapsed off the side of the bed, lips partially open as a whisper of completion seemed to tendril out of it.

William finished his bound with a fall, to all fours, as he stared at her, his mouth open in complete disarray. This, this had to be a nightmare, for truly, he was not robbed of his wife, even as he himself could not control the voice inside of his head. He hadn't had the time to tell her once more how he felt.

It is done my King.

William covered his mouth in horror, realization catching up, as the room seemed to grow darker. Blotches of black filled the outsides of his vision, and a groan escaped him, his mind reeling. Saige was gone. His wife? Abandoned by his wife, how was that love? William shook his head, of course she loved him, and he loved her. Yet, then why did he just waste his last moments as a plaything with the voice?

Why are you, the King, left alone like the discarded Pauper?

Roaring, William stood, spinning as he hurled the nightdesk into the wall, smashing it to bits, storming to the wardrobe to punch it open, watching absentmindedly as his fists and fingers splintered and ripped a hole into the wood, exposing fine linen that too fell sway to his destructive path.

Thrashing and breaking everything in sight, William was lost in a world of dementia and confliction, raging about before finally crumpling at the foot of the bed, rubbing his dead wife's feet, softly whispering to himself, words and phrases she had littered his mind with, at times when things were at its darkest.

"I love you; you know?" William said as tears started to well up in his eyes, voice choking out. "It is only us William, no one else, you see. You are not a monster." Yet even that was short lived as once more despair crashed around him, and he felt his body start to painfully ache, mind jumbled and racing.

Control boy, you must learn control.

The voice was soft now, seeming to hover over him with a caring gesture, ushering him to draw the knife out of its sheath. Doing so, William heard the voice coo once more, and William obeyed, closing his eyes and he ripped apart his tunic, letting the battered rags fall to the ground, placing the knife at the bottom of his stomach.

With a sharp drag, the King drew the knife to the top of his chest, clenching his jaw as he felt the cold taste of steel and the warm flow of blood burst forth, and again he repeated his process. The smell of rust was in the air, as he drug the knife this way, then that, across his chest, then over his arms, then, ripping it across his sides, William noticed as the voice slowly inched forward.

Yes, this is control, my boy. You must never feel the pain of this world, for you are a King. Rest now, rest. I will care for you, and you may sleep, and wash away all the worries and hardships that this world tries to bind you down with. Their chains will never again hold sway.

The voice seemed to gently take over, and William wasn't even mindful as he seemed to fall into a trance, the knife forgotten on the floor as the voice stood, opening the door to where servants stood waiting, eyes opening in slight fear at the blooded image before them.

"Burn the body," the voice said, and William closed his eyes to world, slowly falling back into slumber, only aware of the way the pain of the gashes centralized him.

The voice continued down the halls to where the great door of the keep stood, and flinging it open, it looked about, brisk air scalding his skin, the devilish smile brandishing on his lips looking forced and out of place, like a fish with razor sharp teeth.

Now, the voice thought, it was truly time to play.

Chapter XII
Dante's Book

1790 Anno Domini

William readjusted the cuffs of his sleeves, feeling the embroidery on his skin out of place as he overlooked the forests before him. As he heard the servants bustling behind him, he turned, smiling and offering his welcome to Lady Rosa as she entered the hall of his villa, for the first time since he had known her, forgoing her armor for simple riding pants and wool top, her sword still attached onto her hip as she greeted the King with a curtsy before offering her cheeks.

Behind Lady Rosa stood two young looking men, whose hands were clasped behind their backs as they looked past the King, seemingly without a care as they instead stood resolute behind their Lady. As he watched them, he saw scars around their necks that showed him where they had been collared as slaves, and looking down at Susan, he smiled mischievously, reaching out his arm to the table before the party where his servants were laying food.

"Shall we begin?" William asked, walking Susan to her chair that he pulled out before walking to the other end of the table, where his servant had his own chair pulled out for the King, and as William sat, he watched as the two servant men stood against the wall behind them.

"Most of them answer near unnoticeable cues," Susan said, smiling at William as he studied them and their all too stone appearances. "Others are given a little more leniency while we mold them because as you might imagine, you cannot think for all of them. However, these two are the simplest I needed to show you. If you want to, you can try them out."

William nodded absentmindedly as one of his servants laid the first course in front of him, and savoring a whiff of their wine, started to eat, the clinking of fine china and silver ware echoing across the stone as neither party spoke, the small bustling of the kitchen staff down the hall all too noticeable.

"So," William said, taking a brief glance at Susan where she sat watching him, blowing slowly on the broth in front of her, scar dark under her hair that lay around her face. "Tell me about the adventures outside my Kingdom, surely it is more entertaining than the forgotten King in his quest for the book?" He smiled as he watched her roll her eyes, and wiping his mouth on the cloth, he downed his entire glass of wine, ushering for the servants to bring out the meats.

Susan paused for a moment, staring at William before clicking her tongue and smirked when William watched her two servants turn without a word, exiting the hall, the wooden doors booming shut behind them. "There is a lot that you might not know my King, surely you must find others that can listen and feed you information, I will not be here forever."

William grumbled, tearing apart the meat before him, pouring more wine into his glass as he nodded for Susan to continue, not looking up as he downed yet another glass, loving the feeling of warmth slip down into his belly.

"Lucian is on the warpath, he joined Tirual Acu's family around ten years ago, and has been feeding his entire family information about us." William looked up to Susan with a troubled expression, anger flashing across his face, but Susan raised her hand, stopping the Kings monologue before it came. "I am handling it, don't worry," she paused, watching William's reaction as she reached for the wine.

William reached over, offering her the bottle before settling back into the chair, slicing off another piece of meat as he watched the old commander continue, watching her systematically dice her meal.

"Since you exiled him, he has killed Emily

Damus, the other pit survivor, whom you also exiled," Susan paused as William sat up, annoyance rushing through him as he remembered how skilled of a fighter she had been. Susan continued, eyebrows raised as she carefully moved the knife from her plate to her left-hand side, a few feet away. "He also has killed her husband," Susan paused again, taking a moment to catch her breath, "Christian Santiago, your son."

William scowled, reaching for the bottle once more. "Christian was never my son; he was merely one of my seed who got himself exiled. Although I am sorry to hear of both of their passing's, my bigger concern is what exactly you are going to do about this traitor to the Elder who is now hunting those that have information on us, and offering his knowledge to the services of the family so hell bent on our utter destruction."

Susan smiled, ushering William's servants to bring more food and another bottle, calling for a darker, richer vintage as she set herself to the task of removing the cork as she stood over the table, looking down at the King.

"Our young Asher is my solution,"

William smashed his fist on the table, making the dining set rattle as he pounded it again and finally a third time, clenching his jaw in anger. His voice roared harshly against the walls as it shook the very air,

Susan remaining quiet in his flashed temper. "Asher had the chance to gather the book, along with you might I add, and instead while you were busy with the island and your tasking, he allowed the book to slip past his hands, and even then, failed to kill the guardian of the book. A failed attempt of an Elder if I ever saw one."

Susan continued, unperplexed, her voice softening slightly. "Asher might have failed in grabbing the book like you had wanted in Cuba, but we know now that the book was last seen here, so you are able to take the book for yourself. Although he has failed getting the book however, he has excelled in his other tasks. He has killed the changer Solomon who guarded the book on Cuba and has slain his brother-in-law Ephraim. He has brought it upon himself to slaughter all the men of Acu's bloodline, and from what I can see, he has taken it as a voracious duty, we can rely on him to follow through on his task."

William grumbled, not wanting to acknowledge the success of Asher Valentine, one who he had, himself, deemed so unfit for the Elder. He sat up in his chair, watching Susan carefully as she regarded him, smiling as the scar on her face danced in devilish delight.

"Fine," William admitted, pouring himself yet another glass, as he sat up straighter. "Let us talk about the slaves you brought me. You have pinpointed the book to be in Italy, so in Italy have I staged. Now against the people and the gypsies and those who lurk in the shadows, I have waged war. However, with the changing of times, I need more than just the dwindling Elder. I need an Army."

William leaned back, interlocking his fingers as he regarded Susan's face, as she too leaned back, ushering for the next wave of food, this time a salad, as she quickly readjusted the sword at her hip, flicking her tongue across her lips. "You asked me for humans that would make your causation their own, and indeed have I delivered." She paused, motioning for William's servants to bring back her own, and William watched as her stoned faced servants entered the hall, going right back to the positions at the wall that they had just been, looking past him eerily. "I call them blanks," said Susan, turning herself around in her dining chair to regard her specimens. "They follow any command given to them without hesitation; I used a minor alteration of how you yourself were trained. They are more obedient than soldiers, more primal than courtesans and have less conflictions than slaves. They don't think about their well-being, or garter any connection, they simply live and breathe by your will, which is their peace of mind. They can fight with both weapons of our days, as well as these new technologies, blend in, talk themselves into any estate or castle and are masters at the art of seduction. Simply put, they are the Army that will help you dominate any territory."

William stood, bringing his cup of wine with him as he trailed his fingers across the table, feeling the etchings in the wood as he walked up to the two men, sizing them up as he towered over them. They didn't look up to meet his gaze, or flinch when he leaned in to sniff at them, seeing if they reeked of fear, which they did not. He laughed, clapping one of them on the shoulder before turning to Susan, smiling.

"How many have you brought me then?"

Susan smiled, turning back towards her plate, answering the King as he made his way back to his chair.

"Thirty strong, with a captain of the men to take charge when you are not present."

William rubbed his face, looking once more to the two men, sucking in, *tsking* to Susan. He had wished for more than a paltry thirty soldiers, or blanks as she had called them, however, if they were as good as she said then he would have to oblige. Susan also wasn't one to disappoint, and William knew she had various war tours across the seas before he was more than the Prince, always succeeding at conquering or hiding in a kingdom where their power and influence was needed.

Reaching over to refill her wine glass, he nodded finally, letting her know that he found her offering acceptable. When she caught his eye and smirked, he voiced a few questions that started to run around amok in his mind. "I don't know how long I will be here; how often will my shipments be to replace outdated models? Do they have female counterparts, in case I need them in the man's world? How self-functioning is the captain of the blanks, how long can I leave him and them alone without my command?"

Without skipping a beat, Susan popped a tomato into her mouth, closing her eyes to savor the juiciness that sprang across her mouth as she seemed to relish the finer aspects of dining, thanks to the Kings estate. "I can send you replacements every six months to do with as you will, and if you don't need them, then you can send them back, or put them to work elsewhere. As for making females, I could technically make female counterparts, but you would have to wait for a few years, it is no easy task erasing someone's entire being to replace it with what you want. I will look into it for you however William, and I will send you another captain ever few years, so be sure not to have them die on you; they do what you say and nothing more, unless it is for completion on a mission, you must direct them."

William said nothing, tilting his head quickly in understanding as he poured the last of the wine into his glass, feeling the breeze from the open doors to the outside brush across the back of his neck and his mind wandered as he felt slightly fuzzy from the drink. *Saige*, William thought as he suddenly felt utterly alone in the hall, surrounded by fine things and servants and slaves, all underneath him.

"My King," Susan's voice filled the hall, and he looked up to see her smiling softly. She must have seen the ghost of her daughter in William's mind because he watched as her brows furrowed and she reached across the table to clasp his hands gently, squeezing them quickly. "You need an heir my King, one of your own blood, for even if your reign is longer than anyone can hope for, eventually you will need someone to pass all this onto."

William visibly gagged, going to release his hands from Susan's, but she tightened her hold on his, keeping him bound as she continued. "Just like I have to continue my line with another child, so shall you, don't leave the future of our Kingdom in jeopardy. You never know what the future holds, but in holding your personal future you narrow down the chances of us being expunged from history due to the fading memories. Sleep with a servant, or hell, even one of my blanks I send you, but you must have an heir. Clear your mind from the past."

"How soon will this batch be ready then?" William asked, pulling his hands from Lady Rosa as he picked up his glass, to gulp the wine, savoring the burning in his stomach that ballet against his skin.

Susan remained unperturbed as she herself leaned back, snapping her fingers causing the blanks to finally move from their wall to make their way behind the King, backs against his side of the villa, hands still clasped behind their backs as they stared forward. Susan leaned forward, a devilish grin on her face as she pounded the table. "They are ready at your will my King, I brought all of them with me, but I wonder what you will call them, since you should not have the presence of the Elder known here; surely Acu and his kin already heard the rumors of the book being here."

William whispered, smiling to himself as he versed the supreme poet of Florence, where his estate stood. "Dante's Book."

Chapter XIII
Unleashing

1820 Anno Domini

William strode forward, watching his men in formation to his left, stone faced as he smirked, turning to his right to stare across the distance between another batch of men who were making their way over to the King, and even from here, he was able to see the difference between soldiers and boys trying to play at war. William watched as they finally stopped, the leader of the pack detaching and walking the last fifteen feet to stand in front of William, almost a foot shorter, his ice blue eyes trying to pierce the Kings.

"William," the young man said, offering him his hand that William in turn refused to take, instead, filling the silence with his disproval.

The young man was dressed in brown robes and a cloak, a masquerade mask hanging around his neck in the shape of an eagle. William scanned his body up and down, stripping away any false bravado as he watched the man grow slightly nervous.

"Kale," William said, finally breaking his silence to look past him to where his small cult gathering stood on edge, seeming to watch the King uneasily, as if they knew they couldn't stop him from killing their leader from this distance.

William had met Kale almost eight years ago, when William himself was hunting down the rumors of the Book of Ages, leading him to the western outskirts of the city, where he came upon four teenagers, all garbed in what he mockingly always thought of as costumes. The thieves of Italy, William had scoffed back then, seeing such malleable and weak creatures attempting to will the world to their ways, not realizing that the speck of their existence was already dictated in stone. William had listened to rumors for over thirty years of being in this ancient city, and in those thirty years, William had watched from the shadows, training his men, and intertwining himself into the rumors that often times leaked out of a place so old, unable to hold it in any longer. The city of the damned, full of secrets had treated William kindly, and even as a King from unknown lands, he had played the masterful hand of deceit.

"The city guard will be here shortly, they sent word before we came to meet you here William. The other thieves will be here shortly, so what do you want to do; you are in charge of killing anything, are we still agreed on this?" Kale watched William cautiously, but the King smiled, sinking to his knee as he ran his fingers through the grass, watching the mansion in the distance as Kale harrumphed, walking back to his young men.

William in his patience had known this young man's father, a very nice specimen of a man, whose appearance almost resembled Susan's, with a scar that ran from his neck to his lip, ravaging his face of anything but hatred, who the King had met almost twenty years ago, while taking notes on the man who lived in the mansion the King now kneeled just outside the walls from. For in that mansion lay an old man who went by the name of Tibidabo, and William over time had heard that this thief, this collector of books and boys, had in his possession the one book that truly ever mattered to man, and one that had long thwarted the Kings grasp.

The more the King has sought for information, the more he realized that spread out across Firenze and Fiesole was the man's fiefdom, elaborate schemes, betrayals and mantras laid bare across the lands to subjugate all those under his thumb, and William had no choice but to respect this old man, regardless of the obstacle he tried to waylay the King with, unbeknownst to him. Now, before the King, lay the last efforts of this misted man, to hide the powerful Book of Ages beyond his doors, but the King had laid such schemes of his own to slaughter everything in this city.

Movement in the night caused William to turn on his toes, still kneeling as he watched more shapes emerge from the darkness, and standing tall, the King watched as two more boys and a girl strode forward. These three coming towards the King had also been met over eight years ago while they were but saplings to the willow, however, William saw how even know they had started to fill their forms, and the woman, flanked by the men on both their sides pierced into him with little regard, a doves mask in her left hand, her right lying on the pommel of her hook swords.

"Lynx," William said respectfully, tilting his head down in regards as she said nothing in turn, continuing to watch him.

The King knew she mistrusted him ever since the night they met, and she had good reason too, for before this night was over, the King would have slaughtered every paltry peasant that stood before him, instead of playing to the charade that was just a simple man holding off invaders from the south of Firenze. He was the King, and he would ensure that none of them forgot it.

"Are you prepared William?" Lynx spoke, nodding her head to Kale and the others and William watched as the men started to fall out, shuffling quietly towards the mansion where all the rooms where illuminated. He watched this small woman turn towards him, and William felt a memory flash across his mind of Emily; the pit survivor from oh so long ago.

The King growled. "You asked me privately that you want Tibidabo for yourself, but that book you retrieved from the Cathedral of Pisa, are you *sure* it is there? William regarded the girl dressed in white, her two shining hook swords at her side, and for some reason William felt a sudden wave of familiarity wash over him. His mind flashed to Cuba, where Susan had given the layout of their foes, and had mentioned hook swords there too, but surely this wasn't the same set.

His mind quickly raced to the guild of Italy that laid to the west, the group that was supposed to help them eradicate everyone, and William silently mouthed their name as he turned towards his men, waiting patiently. Six Dragons, did they tie to history of Cuba? Surely, they couldn't be tied to that group from over two hundred years ago.

"My King?" The captain of Williams men was standing in front of him, and William shook his head, clearing the foggy thoughts that started to creep and take root as his normalcy of a scowl appeared.

Looking across the distance, he saw that

all the others had already started making the trek to the mansion, where surely their opposition prepared, and the King signaled to his men, starting to walk towards the most obvious doom that these humans would ever come to know. As he walked, the voice conjured again, quiet over the past decade now that William had invited him wholly in, unsure really of who was who any longer, listening to the slight snake of a voice that whispered to him.

Will we unleash on those that stand before us; shall we kill them?

William smiled, his savagery knowing no bounds as he spoke to his men. His voice was absolute, and he didn't try to hide it as he heard commotion in the fields and house ahead. "Kill everyone here, as instructed. Nobody is to leave this house, regardless of what side they are on. My tasking is my own, leave me to it."

Without a word, William stopped in his tracks, looking over the wall of foliage in front of him where the second story lights were blazing, showing miniature humans converging on themselves, their paltry weapons drawn as they danced antagonizing slow about each other. William scoffed, ushering for his men and captain to continue on ahead of him and listened absentmindedly as they cut their way through the hedge wall that stood before them, as their King stood and watched the figures in the distance, trying to decipher one to the next, yet they were all dressed the same, swarmed with a mountain of books; a library perhaps.

Then William saw it. The Book of Ages being reeled up by what looked like rope, clear as day even from this distance, and William smiled, taking a few steps back, his eyes never shifting from his target. Then suddenly it fell from view and the bookcases started to break and fall, as if the fight was smashing them apart. Growling, he tightened his sword on his hip and then bounded forward, jumping up to the top of the hedge with inhuman accuracy, catapulting from the top of the hedge straight through the glass window of the second floor, bracing against the glass as it shattered, rolling a few feet across the ground.

Standing slowly, William brushed the glass off his chest, noticing a few small cuts on his forearms as he saw Lynx in front of him, staring at another thief, garbed as a Raven, his mask, and clothes immaculately splendid. The King eyes slowly trailed to his sword, and smiling he strode forward boldly, leaping over Lynx to stand in front of this opponent, noticing him as the person who had just had the Book of Ages moments before.

"Where is the book boy!" The King roared, feeling his spine start to buzz with energy as hatred sprang to form across his body.

The boy didn't answer, instead cowering slightly as he seemed to recoil from a nightmare, he had no idea could exist. William quick as a flash pounced forward, picking up the boy still lost for words, throwing him through the air to smash into the wall, creating a hole that he became stuck in, and the King smiled devilishly, walking slowly forward as he regarded his prey like the insect he was.

"Everyone will know that you were killed by William Santiago, the King of the Elder."

William watched as the boy feverishly scrambled, trying to escape from the wall as he watched William starting to bear down on him, and the King could smell the stench of fear fill the room. The raven boy finally escaped just as William closed the distance, falling to all fours, gasping for breath and William smiled, reaching down to grab him by his throat, lifting him high in the air, the Kings grip tightening like a vice as the boy's feet kicked manically in the air, fingers trying to unlock the Kings around his throat.

Smiling, William saw as the boy's eyes started to bulge, his face turning blue like a blueberry ready to burst. In what seemed to be a last resort, the boy brought his fancy masks beat crashing down on the Kings wrist, but William didn't flinch, instead chortling as his voice came out in a mocking tone, tightening his grip further still, almost to the point of breaking his neck.

"Such a weak fellow you are," William said, his voice coming out in a low growl and patronizing tone.

Then with a surprise, the boy stabbed his fingers into the Kings eyes and William roared, eyes flashing with bright lights as he forced them closed, pain flashing across him as he spun and threw the boy like a ragdoll, caring not where he landed as he felt for his eyes, feeling them watering as he felt as if they had been struck with a fire poker.

Turning with a flash, William growled animalistically, eyes closed as he started forward, following the scent of the boy like a hound hunting a rabbit cowered in the bush. Sniffing gently, William took two steps forward in the direction of where he knew the boy lay on the floor, most surely frozen in fear, but then the King stopped, and he snapped his head to the right where he heard people burst through a door of the library, and the wind from the window carried a new scent across to the King.

Death.

Before the King had time to prepare, he felt a force slam into him, spinning agilely around the larger man's body so he was on the Kings back, arm wrapped around his throat as a second force barreled into his stomach, moving his a few feet back as William reached out blindly to grab his assailants, stopping his movement back as he snarled loudly. Their stench of death filled his nostrils, and William knew that these were Tiraul Acu's men, Vampires in the flesh.

William grabbed the arm wrapped around his throat, and threw with behemoth force, sending one of them crashing into the wall as William roared, bringing his knee up to smash into the face down by his waist, and as the man roared, standing up William kicked forcefully, sending the man back to fall on the ground, giving William some needed space.

"William Santiago," a voice said off to his right, and his skin prickled up as if a winters breeze ran across his skin. "It is here that the King of the Elder will find his end, long forgotten amidst men. Are you prepared to meet your Gods?"

William opened his eyes, looking at the three men in front of him, taking in their gray tunics and veils covering their faces, seeing their ashen skin and dark eyes as they slowly started walking forward in unison, converging onto William who smiled, untying his sword from his hip as he dropped it to the library floor, a twinkle in his eye as he felt the coiled power in his spine.

"Francis, Arthur and Almari," the King

said, taking a step back as he grasped a shelf of a bookcase, his eyes fluttering as he concentrated, releasing the power that was always threatening to come out. "I am happy to see Acu has not gotten soft in his old age, I wish you slow and painful deaths."

He unleashed the entirety of the power, screaming harshly as his body racked with convulsions, making the King fall to his knees, eyes screwed and slitted, but open as he watched the three paused in their advancements as he saw the youngest looking one look worried over to the white-haired Francis. Again, the King bent under the pressure before a black curtain drifted over his eyes and the beast released itself, standing from the ground as the terror of the Elder. The beast rose, clothes tattered rags forgotten on the floor as it stood to its full height, nine feet tall, covered in fur as its arms hung almost to the floor, claws six inches long dragging on the floor. The King growled, his animal-self moving forward as he bared his teeth, fangs covered in saliva as he roared, yellow eyes piercing his prey in the room as he pounced forward into the throng of the three men.

The King of the Elder, of the Werewolves slashed at them, sending them scattering as they drew weapons, and almost catching one, the beast's jaw snapped shut in thin air, hoping that his fangs would rip an unsuspecting victim, but wasn't so lucky. He roared as he felt white fire sear into his thigh, and turning, smashed apart the wooden shaft of the lance that protruded from him. He leapt onto Almari, the youngest of the three, pinning him under his force, biting into his shoulder, ripping out large chunks of flesh before he leapt away, spinning to face the other two who had their weapons out, veils forgotten as their deathly countenance emanated across the library.

Just as Francis opened his mouth to speak, a flutter of movement made him turn, and the beast growled happily as Asher entered the room, looking travel weary and spent, his hair all about his face, his famous knife out and facing the two still standing Vampires, Almari writhing as the venom of the beast seeped into his bite, keeping him indisposed.

"Just in time I see," Asher said menacingly, nodding to the King as he mockingly bowed to Francis. "Now, which of you is to die first?"

Carnage, thought the voice as the beast of the King started forward slowly, discarding the lance behind him, tinkling on the ground before it laid still. *We will kill them all!* The beast and Asher pounced between their ambushed prey.

Chapter XIV
New Beginning

1840 Anno Domini

The King paced through the halls of his villa, aware of how quiet it had gone as the whispering of the winds off the trees brushed against his face as he gazed down at the vineyards below, a desolate courtyard in front of him, vines entangling up the columns of his once mighty estate. The book had never resurfaced, even after the deaths of those humans had inked away in history, still the King could not find the book, nor any whisper of where it had gone. How had he lost this chance, and how could someone hide something so important from *him*, the King!

He turned quickly, tearing a tapestry off the wall and watched angrily as it fluttered to the ground, his nostrils flared as his nose twitched, face set in a scowl as he heard Asher enter the hallway, silent in his consideration of his Master, fine clothes on his body, a crimson brooch at his neck in the shape of a sword and a rose, the sigil of the Elder.

"Our carriage is awaiting to carry us to our transportation my King."

Asher regarded him only a moment longer, until he looked up at him, half ways giving him a glance of annoyance, and Asher bowed, stepping back before turning to leave the King alone in his tantrum.

Walking back to face the open courtyard, he could see the horse drawn carriage in the distance, the dust of the movement starting to cloud up as it made its way towards where the King stood and watched it, like a final pose of the failure of his legacy. He snarled once more before he turned to walk towards the main hall where his few remaining servants stood in line, his goods and luggage laid in front of them as they waited for his word to move it to the front door.

As he entered the hall, he silently regarded them as they began to shuffle about in confusion and nervousness. Never had the King just sat and stared at them in prolonged distaste, and now that he had, he felt a small wrenching in his stomach as his mouth started to salivate. However, before saying a word, Asher stepped up behind the King, clapping his hands twice as the servants shook out of their thoughts and started to cart the Kings belongings past him, making sure not to scuff up or demark the remaining items in the main hall; one of the girls giving the King a sideways glance, seeming to regard him with a sorrowful expression.

"Once all of my things have been loaded up, I want you to slit their throats. We have no need to have rumors of the Elder to stay in this area of the world once we have left, nor do we need words traveling to our enemies." The King spoke absolutely, without even glancing at Asher to see if he had any objections, instead continuing down to the private staircase where the King could walk the remains of his villa in peace.

Asher's voice called out against the main hall, echoing eerily as it was absorbed by nothing but the stones. "All of them?"

"All but the female blank," the King said gruffly, closing the door behind him with a boom before pausing for a moment.

He staggered over to a window, holding his arms out on each side of it as his head swam in a rush of thoughts, knees growing weak as the King laid his head on the cold touch of the glass pane, screwing his eyes shut as pain sprouted in between them. *Saige.* The King growled as he screwed his shut even tighter, smacking his left hand hard onto the stone as a vocal growl issued deadly through his teeth, a shimmer of power rolling up his spine. *Saige.*

The voice roared, rearing back as he struck his fist through the window to erase the thoughts. The voice could feel William trying to escape his hold, slowly using his last remnants of a forgotten age to conjure up a counterattack to the iron-like vice grip that the voice held William in. Yet, try as he might, a vision again appeared in his host's head, and the voice had no power to keep it away, growling as he watched in anger, slowly trying to tighten the bonds once more.

William watched her from the windowsill, laying his forehead on the pane as the rain peltered down, the cool flash of the glass running through his face as he watched the muddied gray of the world on the outside. He could see the people in the streets walking about their life's, some running in the rain, sure to escape to their cozy little spells of warmth of hearth while others just seemed to become giddy and run and dance in jubilance with whomever they were with. William turned back to Saige to see her at the corner desk, drawing pad opened, her nose an inch from the paper as she scribbled furiously, her fingers starting to smudge by her art, hair laid over her shoulder to one side, showing him her care free as lax in emotion, save her eyes.

The voice countered, opening his eyes to the desolate and dark encroachment that was threatening not only the house, but the grounds; the sky itself turning upon itself as the clouds seemed to grow dark in the God's wrath, threatening to swallow up the land in a flood. The voice felt William recoil to the cold, feeling a twinge of pain.

You were but a spectator to her kindness, like a young and foolish boy who had been sent to the shop to gather sweets, fully aware that you were regarded in kindness simply because you offered business. Or perhaps it was the proper way. You were but a guest in the world, and as a guest shall you remain, for that is what you were only ever made to be. You were made, and now in your making you will be a subjugated fool to life, with a countenance of loneliness, berift of any choice to make yourself. You are but a King by my own hand, and in my own hand will you ensure that the Kingdom remains.

The voice finished speaking, closing his eyes to breath slowly through his nose. Quiet. The King opened his eyes as he smirked, quickening his pace down the steps to where yet another passage led him to the front entrance. It was there that the carriage was pulling to a stop, the horses whinnying as the servants started loading luggage onto the back, Asher watching to ensure nothing was out of place from atop his own horse, looking almost regal before bile rose in the Kings throat, his lip curling.

Besides Asher, the King watched as the blanks also looked on, in perfect formation, eyes unblinking as they seemed to take everything in, and as the King approached them, the Captain stepped forward, face expressionless as he waited for a command to be given to him. Slowly the King drew the man's own knife from its sheath, and the Captain looked down, still not responding as he regarded the King coolly.

"Slay all your men, save the woman. That is your last command."

The King heard Asher and his horse trot behind him, and for a brief moment, the King saw something flicker in the blank man's face, something like the breaking of years of conditioning, but nodding, the Captain turned and quickly walked up behind his men, slicing their throats open as the men started to gurgle and drop to their knees, the blood spurting sickeningly far as they fell completely to the ground, feeding the dry earth with the last any human had to offer. As he finished, the Captain turned back to the King, jaw clenched, and the King smiled mischievously.

"Asher," the King said expectedly, and Asher dropped from his horse, quickly grabbing the man by his collar, shoving him against the stone of the Kings villa, stabbing him through the underside of his jaw, the King watching with a smile as his light dimmed from his eyes before finally Asher released the now lifeless sack of flesh, turning to the only blank left, the woman, offering his hand to her.

"The King asks for you to join him in the

carriage on this voyage, should you be so inclined." The King listened to the silver tongue that Asher seemed to have gotten from his father Benjamen as he saw the blank give a flicker of a nod before he escorted her to the carriage to wait upon the King.

Finally, when all seemed to be ready to begin their travels, the King laid his hand on Asher's shoulder, watching him carefully as he whispered from ears that could hold secrets not meant to be heard. "When we reach the ship, leave your horse. I want the two of us to reach the shores of the Americas without anything holding us apart or down to do what we have to do. You did send out the message to the other vassals of the Elder, correct? Susan and the like will meet us there?" The King spoke quickly, and watched as Asher nodded his head, stating that everything was fully taken care of, showing no hint of betrayal.

"Your will and your Elder will endure and prosper on the new shores of wherever you take us," Asher said, turning to mount his horse as he nodded towards the carriage, a twinkle in his eyes. "Your servant awaits her handler."

Saige.

The King growled, turning to take the few steps to where the blank sat, watching him, eyes piercing him like a hunter. *Saige is rotting under the ground because you could not save her, any less than she would be able to save you from yourself. Impudent children run to someone for the iniquities of the soul that they themselves wholeheartedly embraced. Pauper.*

The King spit on the ground as William was forced to quiet again, and opened the carriage door, he got in, watching the female blank as he knocked on the door of the carriage, signaling to their transporter that they were ready, and with a small jerk, the carriage was off, leaving the old city, and the old ruins of Italia in the background as they went on their way to the new world, and the ship that awaited them on the shores.

The blank watched the King apprehensively the more he stared at her with a hungerous look, and finally she asked what it was that the King wanted to have her do when they moved to their next house. Her next assignment before he too found her to be replaceable, slaying her where she stood. Yet the King didn't seem to register the emotion in her voice, instead looking out of the window, tapping his temple forcefully as he muttered to himself, growling before he laid his hand back onto his lap, face going dead flat.

"The Elder will go and conquer the new world, for surely that is where our enemies are now flocking to. We will go and we will ensure that our histories are not forgotten that our war is not over until they are all slain and buried under the ground. In this new world we will thrive, and you, you will bring me an heir. One to take up my mantle while my Kingdom encompasses all the lands across the world."

Chapter XV
Redemption

1864 Anno Domino

"They are ready for you, my King." William turned slowly to face Susan as she regarded him with a look of understanding, the wrinkles starting to conjure on her skin, a comparison likened to William's soul.

Let us rejuvenate you.

William flinched, his breathing slowing down as he held onto the bannister before him. Finally escaping the labyrinth of his mind, William had grown quiet, often times lost in daydreams and memories that people around him seemed unable to notice. Now the days of his existence seemed to be spread thin, his mind like an overaged wine, left to spill on cobblestone, long forgotten.

"William?" Susan offered a hand on his shoulder, curiosity and care etched into her face as she helped him stand to his full height.

Flanking on her either side was her daughter Lily, who she had brought up after she had left the King in Italy, and from there, stood Susan's granddaughter, Michaela, a fresh adult in both man's eyes, and the eyes of the Elder. She was short like her mother Lily, and while Lily had a different father than Saige, some of the genes from Susan had moved to Lily, and while they weren't identical, Lily still looked easily as Saige's sister.

Michaela on the other hand reminded William like Emily, all sprightful and rebellious, even her hair cut in pixie like fashion, angling her facial features even more, making her cat like gaze even more nerve wracking.

William grumbled, moving forward towards the birthing room, feeling Susan's hand on his back, almost propelling him forcefully forward, keeping him from backpedaling away from the ones that awaited him on the inside of the room.

The room was lighted, unlike the other times in the past he had witnessed the birthing of a child, and William audibly gasped when he saw the baby girl, swaddled and wrapped, her ocean blue eyes seeming to capture the very skies in her irises, as she cooed and babbled at William when he had walked in.

"Alecia," William said, striding forward, inattentive to anyone else in the room as his focus anchored on this child that he reached down to bring into his arms, her hand around his thumb, staring focused and then unfocused at her father who face broke into a smile never seen before.

William lifted Alecia up so that they were face to face, and her smile hovered in front of him, and he was able to see the flicker of her mouth as she stared at him, dimples showcasing as she rested her chubby cheeks in hand.

She was a beauty, one that William had no trouble seeing, but yet he felt a small twinge of remorse and guilt. She was not the child of the woman he loved, or was it hated? The memories were torn from his mind and warped as ages passed; the demons whispering so loudly now that sometimes his words were not his own. But this child, this girl, truly was a marvel, a proper Princess for the Elder, one who he knew would take after him and be strong and commanding. He needed to ensure it happened, and in that moment, his mind cleared.

He remembered what life was, instead of how he interpreted it. She reminded him of what love should be, and how passion felt. When she moved, the stirring in him showed him everything he thought he had lost.

She gave him hope.

Looking over to Susan, he nodded to her, before turning on his feet, going to leave the birthing room, without giving a second glance to the female blank he had left on the bed, and as the door slowly shut, he heard Susan unsheathing her sword.

He carried the newborn daughter down the hall to where his advisors had been waiting, and all save the Rosa entourage were not present. Thunderous applause stampeded through the room, and Asher was seen standing with a toast amongst the other Elder who had been present since the late Queen Mother was still alive.

"It is today that Alecia Santiago, the noble of the Elder; the Princess of everything we have and everything we will have! On this day, the enemy quakes in fear at what she will achieve, and the men shiver to behold her magnificent beauty!"

William smiled, looking down at his daughter, feeling faces all about him, and a shiver ran into his jaw. Unconsciously glancing up to the corner of the room, in the corner of his eye, he saw the misted voice sitting, seeming to recoil in disgust and despair at the sight of the Kings daughter.

More people to watch you fail, and even worse, have you fail them.

Susan and her kin walked into the room, and immediately, William felt as Lily reached for his daughter, cooing and smiling as the bundle of flesh was taken from his arms and spirited out of his reach before Susan stood on Williams right hand side, her granddaughter Michaela on his left, Asher silencing the chamber for the

Misses. Susan spoke first, reaching over to grab a glass of champagne that had awaited the other visitors in the chamber, while Alecia was being born. Downing it, she began.

"We have been a part of this new world for some time now; in the last thirty years we have helped to shape some of the doctrine in the world of man, yet also in the world of the undertow. Gangsters and spies, rats and thieves have sought and learned from us just as much as the politicians and the coppers, the teachers, and the Doctors. Yet in the coming years, as Acu and his men keep pouring over, our war will exceed anything we have seen since before even William himself was born." Susan paused, looking around the table and then to William who nodded, filling the quiet with his loud and deep voice, feeling strong in the moment, absent-mindedly feeling more drained than ever before.

"Acu and his men are ever expanding their hold, their search for advancements and artifacts never-ending in their totality. Unlike us, they truly live forever, unless we kill them, and the days of our oldest members are drawing to a close. Soon, even the great Lady Rosa will pass, and who do we have to offer in her place? In the place of the armies we have, or the battle-hardened Lords. We have naught but man, and naught but children, untrained and sculpted into any significant force. This must change."

With a chorus of here-here's, Asher raised his hand to silence the room, questioning William expectantly as his mouth opened and his father's voice rang out, causing William to flicker in distaste. "If you are speaking about mass training, and using others as the fodder of war, then truly you have a plan for those of us, like myself, who have fought battles in the unseen trenches, relying more on spy craft than formations and orders. Is the new world too good for the old guard?"

Michaela Rosa spoke up, her eyes sparkling with a light of fury that William had never seen in any of the Rosa woman, save Susan, and William smiled inwardly, thanking Susan for crafting such good kin.

"Our King has asked myself, as well as a few others who finished the initiation into the Elder with me, to work on a sub branch that would work in the shadows of the Elder, offering the information that we learn, but also giving us the freedom to do with our movements what we will. Our King is not disbanding the old guard, because the old guard is what keeps the elder going. However, in this day and age, if Acu is truly tempting others with the promise of immortality, and if the army that he gathers at our gates is truly too big to handle, than surely it would make sense to have an army of your own that works outside the frameworks of the Elder, one that can combat them at recruiting, and help even one as sly as you Sir Valentine, at retrieving information."

The chamber was silent, all eyes looking expectantly up to William, who in turn leaned down to brace himself on the table, taking in the battle formations and the plans that lined on top of the table and watched as Susan's gauntleted hand banged and then rested on the side.

"The last time all of us were brought together, King William Santiago was born. In that time, the late Queen Mother directed and commanded our armies across the world, yet she also sent me secretly with my Hunters to change the course of history. If now fate dictates us all to come together again, at the birth of the Princess, then surely it is fate itself dictating that my granddaughter and others should start their own hunting party, under another name, to carry out our will; a sword to slay with the Kings mighty sigil. Are any of us to object?"

The chamber was silent once more, and without objections, William stood, nodding to Michaela, and then Asher and Susan. Looking at each of the Lords in the room, he smiled, picking up a piece from the table, a muddied gray piece, before he snapped it in half within his large hand.

"Acu and his men are our targets, and the Book of Ages is our key to success. In this new world, we will bring the old guard and the old ways to stamp our sigil into the pages of history until everyone knows who commanded it."

Alecia babbled in the background, and the King turned, smiling even fiercer as he reached for his tiny little Princess, the noble of the Elder.

Chapter XVI
The Mist

1871 Anno Domini

William strode forward through the streets of the town, twirling the pocket watch round and round as he brought his sword cane forward to crunch into the dull cobblestone, the smoke from the coal yards filtering across the streets, choking the sunlight away. All around him, passersby tipped their hats to him, yet William could see the silent judgement of his skin colour, or the sheltered fear chipping away at their soul as they quickened their pace, hoping that today was not the day that he spoke to them, demanding information or work to be done; this was his city, his kingdom. Another clink of his cane, then another, slowly watching the humans live their lives, some even paying him no attention as they surely weren't aware of the deeper machinations of the government of their lands and life.

"Just around the corner here my King," said a voice over his right shoulder where

Michaela was following him, looking out of place in the dress she wore, with a matching grimace on her face that William was sure was on his.

However, he had to admit that even in the out of place wardrobe, Michaela did dress up nicely, and even in this city, the whispers of her beauty were always the stuff of whispered secrets and wanting. She had the eyes to crumble any nation of old, and her voice, albeit not like the silver tongue of Asher, was a golden blanket, quick to entangle and ensnare any unhappy prey. Besides the senior Lady Rosa, Michaela was the epitome of centuries of collective knowledge and breeding, until now, when she was destined to be the right hand of the Elder, to take her mother's place and serve alongside Williams' own daughter.

"What are these humans like then, is there anything I should know, going in?" William's voice was quiet, the hubbub of the bustling people and cars starting to roar louder to life as Michaela and he reached closer to the center of the city.

"Not really no, they have been in communication with me, mainly through the post after our original meeting. They simply want to meet the King of our people, so in the future of this city, they are able to live freely with the knowledge of who we are, and with respect, garter the same respect of allowing them to coexist next to us in the city we call our home. All in all, they are a pretty grim but young lot, I expect you will enjoy them as much as I have."

William gave her a sideways glance, the corners of his mouth raising a fraction as he gave her a sly smile before looking again once ahead, nudging her with his elbow, chortling quietly. "Now now Michaela, you know our rules in the Elder, you are not to grow an attachment of any sort from someone who is not in our group. If your grandmother finds you prepared for a husband, she will find you the perfect match, both in specimen and mind, a proper fit that even you could not find issue with. Be careful that she doesn't hear about whatever games you find yourself playing with these humans."

Michaela scoffed, going to smack the Kings elbow, but airily missed, clearly aware not to push her luck with him. However, she finally sighed, agreeing with William, her voice falling back into the razor edge that had so predominated her countenance while working in the Elder; deadly and absolute. "I know William, I know. Merely a distraction in the constant work life I have tasked before me, besides," she paused, giving the King a doe eyed expression, the shadowy gray eyes of her pixie like face making the hair on the back of his neck rise. "Besides, you'll always be my number one.”

At those words, a couple men trailing behind them harrumphed and cleared their throats, and the King, looking over his shoulder at them, saw them sizing up both he and Michaela, as if she was an escort following a just liberated slave through the streets of their esteemed town.

Rip out their throats my King.

Williams eyes rolled back into his head quickly, a powerful shudder running up his spine as he turned on the spot, facing the men who stood below him, their eyes opening in quick horror as he bared his teeth, licking the corner of his lip as his nose scrunched in anger. However, before he could take a step forward, he remembered his daughter Alecia, and how she sat at the estate, barely seven years old. It would not do justice to lose control in the center of town.

He stared at them a moment longer, watching as they seemed to sink inside of their overcoats, trying to bury their reek of fear, as if it would help. Then turning, he quickened his pace, Michaela trying to keep up, silent now, as if she waited for William to chide her for her silly and out of place remark, yet no remark came from the King, instead he focused on the directions he had received earlier.

Finally he stopped outside a doorstep of what looked like a barbershop, and looking to Michaela, she resoundingly nodded, stepping past the King to open the door, a chime of a bell and an elderly gentleman greeting them as he carefully slide his blade across the face of his client in the chair, wiping off the excess cream on his apron, before nodding to the wall off to his left.

"Just knock there kind Sir, they are expecting you down in the meeting room, be sure to leave all non-essentials up here and the like." The old man paused, seeing Williams look of disbelief at the mere mention of going unarmed, albeit in a what surely could be a basement of humans with weapons. "Just a precaution chap, your disposition precedes you, and to be quite honest, you scare the hell out of them."

William smiled, walking up to the gentleman to lay his heavy hand on his shoulder, leaning down to gaze into his wrinkled face, eyes level as he regarded him insightfully, trying to read his intentions. His deep voice came out gnarled and grinding, purposely allowing his voice to rumble through the air. "I am the weapon chap."

Hearing Michaela off to his right knocking on the wall, William stood, watching the man out of the corner of his eye as he watched the wall split open, opening a crack as a head stuck out, his glasses threatening to fall off his face as he eyed the two Elder in front of him. He hesitated only for a moment before disappearing from view, pushing the hidden door open wider, ushering the King and Michaela inside graciously, eyes darting around them, as if expecting hidden assassins in the corner ready to pull him from his hole.

"We are most grateful that the Elder graces us with their presence. Thank you very much for offering us this chance to sit and discuss at the same table." His voice was reedy, like a man who had lost it from being absent from interactions with another soul, and William wrinkled his nose as he walked in the doorway, seeing stairs precede down before him, into the dark.

Three men awaited them, standing in the shadowed room, clustered around a round table, watching the two Elder descend the final steps until finally they stood level with their hosts, who now sat in unison, smiles on their faces as they gestured to the remaining two seats at the table. William waited a moment longer, watching as Michaela sat down first, smoothing the wrinkles in her dress as she took off her hat and laid it on the tables surface, keeping her eyes on the three men as William followed suit, sitting and then leaning forward on his elbows to regard the three before him.

They were dressed all in similar fashion, each looking masterful in their own right, piercing eyes skating over William's demeanor, seeming to smile mischievously, and William had a touch of concern start to knot into his stomach, swallowing expectantly as the man closest to him finally spoke, moving his gaze to Michaela, who he then offered a genuine smile to.

"My name is Septimus," and gesturing to the two other men besides him, he continued, voice proud. "This is who we call Octavious and Novenus. Through time, we have passed along our names and our teachings, ensuring that our networking and influence follows wherever we decide to dock, into our newest homes. We asked to finally meet the King of the Elder because even if you don't know of us, we have known about you for a long time, always a whisper our mentors passed one to another, ever since Cuba where you rid us of rats, we had helped train."

The man named Novenus gave William a knowing look, quiet as their eyes met and William saw him wink as Septimus continued, drawing the Kings attention back to him, the knot in his stomach growing slightly larger as he caught himself tensed up, as if ready to jump out of his chair.

"We had sent our men there for an artifact that we know that you have been hunting as well," pausing as he leaned forward, as if to share a secret. "The Book of Ages, where it was being hidden by a group of people who had long thwarted us ever since our first run in with them in our histories' past. Thankfully, once they had seduced our own men and women to their ways, along comes the Elder in their magnificence, killing one of our best, and sending a carnal killer after another, hunting him across time until he finally cornered his prey."

Michaela looked questioningly at William, and he looked at her, eyes open in worry. He could not explain it, but something was seriously wrong, and Michaela, not being born during the Cuba crisis, had no idea what was going on, seeing the Kings concern on his face, nodding her head slightly as she straightened up, eyes piercing into Septimus commandingly addressing him.

"We are here to talk about the future of the city, and our working in unison towards common goals. We are not here to talk about the past of the Elder and those who were the namesakes of yours from days since long laid in dust. Let us get to the point and reach a deal so we can all be on our merry ways."

Septimus scowled at Michaela, but Octavious smiled, laughing heartily, slapping his counterpart on the back. "As always, Michaela says the truth, we came here all together to get the point of what we can do for each other, and the limits thereof in perfect synchronization, good girl," he said, giving a small wink to Michaela, who flushed, before continuing, addressing William. "You came here for the Book of Ages we imagine, and we want to know what you plan to use it for, because we are also looking for it, and our reasons are to free this world from lack of knowledge, so they as a race might step forward into the new age."

William stood forcefully, his chair flying to the floor a few feet behind him, hands in fists on the table, bearing down on the three men who sat patiently and unflinching at the sudden tension in the air as he bared his teeth. "The Book of Ages will belong to the Elder, and the Elder alone. We aren't here to banter words with those that are beneath us about items of such magnificence that they cannot even begin to comprehend. We began this journey long before you or your very first namesakes were even born, and we alone will decide what to do with the item that we ourselves will find. I thought your group might have learned that lesson in Cuba, or anyone else for that matter; we will remove anyone from our way who stands between us and our objectives."

He stood up straight to his full height, breathing in deeply as he regarded them coolly, gesturing for Michaela to follow suit, turning to face towards the stairs out of the basement, a shudder running up his spine as he froze in the spot, staring at the shadows that started to move from the corners, blocking his escape.

Francis, Arthur and Almari barred his path, two women flanking on either side of the three men, all garbed in outfits from this age, veils covering their faces even in the dark of the basement. One of the women stepped forward, removing her veil as she regarded William almost sadly, seemingly scanning him head to toe, her eyes woeful as she spoke to him, still in the dark. "William Santiago," she said slowly, drawing two sabers from her sides. "My name is Angel Moore, but back when you were on Cuba, I was called Angel Flint, the lover of the changer that you had Asher hunt down."

William snarled, feeling Michaela on his left side, buzzing with frenzied energy as the men still sat behind them, silent and fearless.

They plotted for this to happen, my King.

"I don't want you to think they were talking to you William," Francis said, his ashen face looking just as old and poisonous as it did back in Italy. His voice was quiet and decrepit as he continued, watching William start to shake with power. "They were speaking to us, for unlike the Elder, we will find the Book of Ages, and unlike the Elder, we will not disappear into nothingness as the new century turns over the old.”

William heard the three men behind him rise from their chairs, and William’s stomach churned angrily. Without looking at her, William grabbed Michaela by the shoulder, bringing his mouth to her ear, keeping his eyes on the vampires blocking his way warily, hearing the men step closer and closer.

“You must run Michaela, get back to the compound. Gather who you will, alert the guard, and keep Alecia protected. I will be here waiting for the Elders return, but you must do this for me without hesitation, and be quick about it.”

He released her without waiting for a reply, stepping forward to mockingly bow to those who stood before them. Standing tall, he started to remove his coat, allowing it to drop to the floor with a flutter, smiling at those who smiled back. “I think the line ages past was which of you is to die first?” William said, shrugging off his shirt as he felt spiraling power roll up his spine as he spun on the spot, knocking out the light of the lantern, throwing the room in complete darkness.

The King snarled, releasing both the voice and the animal, bowing to the ground in the confusion and chaos, shuddering and convulsing as the power almost rent his body in two, his limbs elongating as his pores bled with the pressure, body changing into the nightmare that the world had wanted this whole while before growling, standing in the dark as his piercing yellow eyes made out shapes and shadows, watching as Michaela escaped from behind them, securing them all in the depths below.

Epilogue
Memento

*P*eople always seemed to misunderstand those imbued with a lonely soul; oft fearing the emptiness of that voided canvas of dreams and destiny. They mistook it all as a loss of hope, instead of the realization of the truth: all life came to an end, and for some, there was no lightening the burden of their soul. Where some gave way to fear and dread, others saw the simple resounding promise and trust that surely one day they will rest forever. To greet Death as a friend, signing away your adventure and Honour to one who had long been waiting to see the signature of your heart sketched in blood with a final line of resounding courage. To fear death was to simply not understand it, and why it is the last thing awaiting the end of a journey long withheld from the storytellers.

Yet, pain sprouts from misfortune of anger and greed, wrapping around your ankles. Out of love, anger befalls you. Out of lust, greed creeps into you. Through gray clouds, the silver lining is sometimes hard to see, yet it reaches to all, the touch of the heavens *upon its tendrils. For life itself is simple. A simple breath and a simple process that can be done again and again with little regard. The woes, the choices and the path create meaning, causing hardship or hope. Death is hard: to find meaning and create cause and justice, yet know in the end, your personal dreams unfulfilled are lost to the world. The burning of one's eternal soul to serve deaths justice, while honorable, is conflicted with the burning of one's soul in general; yet all flames must burn out.*

"I knew you would be the one to end it," William said, a small smile coming to his lips as Arthur walked forward with ease, his graying skin and smell making William look away, four scattered bodies of the humans and Francis around him, the four other vampires surrounding him, hurt, yet alive.

"She left me alone with it," he said, looking up at Arthur, confusion written across his face as William continued, unperturbed in his openness at death's doorway. "With my demon. She made me promise to win, so win I shall. I am not like you. I am not weak!"

The King snarled, pouncing from his knees, but he knew he wasn't going to try. The voice had taken everything from the King. Power, people, and property. Even the control of the King himself.

Swords lanced through his calves, pinning him to the ground as Arthur seemed to regard him sorrowfully, yet in that sorrow,

William spat, blood bubbling across the man's pristine clothes.

"Kill me," he said bitterly, the small boy found in his head, weeping, and begging to make it quick. His voice came out in a whisper, a choked sobbed as he remembered the pit of his youth when he had first joined the Elder, his namesake.

"Please."

William thought of Saige in that moment, how he had loved her until the end, enduring long past when the taste of food had become ash in his mouth. It was the cruel movements of fate to have cursed him with a trial unable to comprehend and defeat, his soul turned forever twisted between good and evil. He had long been bound for Hell, which he knew in time would come, to penance for his immortal life of sin, however, for those brief moments of sanity, he had tasted Heaven with her.

He had no hopes while growing up to having the misfortune of love, whether falling into it or finding others to share it with him. Ever since the beginning, since the chamber of lessons, William had long foregone the hope for his paradisiacal Saviour and bereavement of pain and promised to always ensure he sat in the shadows of his soul to ensure that Hell was his only option; yet one he chose for himself. To be free from the shackles of the proverbial Devil.

However, in his folly William had

overestimated the evil of the world, and the candor of his soul insomuch as to believe that he could never love, or that even with all his flaws and mishaps of the mind, someone could give their heart to him, even if he didn't know what that meant. So, when she had found him, he was petrified in the core of his being, all semblance of reality rushed out for a moment pause, and in that limitlessness of time he knew that he loved her.

It wasn't as easy as breathing, the likes of which everyone spoke of. It was shards of glass with every moment around her, he needed to breathe and gladly accepted the pain it caused him from his demons as punishment for being weak to them. The trust and loyalty were absolute, yet he couldn't let anyone know for fear of it being used against him, as the weakness he often sought in others.

His love for her was the answer to everything he wanted to learn from when he was a small boy. Yet sadly for her, she and him both knew that it had arrived many years too late, so only a taste of peaceful contentment was ever given to him. His torment in life was a simple taste of what awaited him in his purgatory full of vigorous reactions to his complacent or obsessive actions.

And in that brief moment of absolute clarity before the closing curtain finished the story of his soul, a tear rolled down his face as he gently bit his lip and closed his fluttering eyes in torturous despair. He had failed everyone, himself included. In the pursuit of power and control, he had lost himself utterly and in furtherance of strife, lost Sage and the weight of the world crushed down on him until a shuddering breath of broken dreams escaped his lifeless body.

About the Author

Dorian P. Belasko is an author of historical fantasy for adults and teens, including his upcoming YA debut, The Monster Within. He was born in Chatan-Cho, Naha Province, Japan, and has traveled most of his life - finally settling down in Florida. When not writing, he can be found on the beaches of the Caribbean, the Jungles of Southeast Asia, or getting lost in the beauty of the Greek Isles - all before returning to the comfort of a bookstore or library, where he soaks up the texture and the scent of old moth-riddled stories.